MW00592578

Eagle Nest Bayou

Roger Jones

To Jim
&
Fran

Roger

06-27-08

Copyright © 2008 by Roger Jones

*All rights reserved. No part of this book shall be repro-
duced or transmitted in any form or by any means,
electronic, mechanical, magnetic, photographic including
photocopying, recording or by any information storage and
retrieval system, without prior written permission of the
publisher. No patent liability is assumed with respect to
the use of the information contained herein. Although
every precaution has been taken in the preparation of this
book, the publisher and author assume no responsibility for
errors or omissions. Neither is any liability assumed for
damages resulting from the use of the information
contained herein.*

*This is a work of fiction. Names, characters, places, and
incidents either are the product of the author's imagination
or are used fictitiously. Any resemblance to actual events
or locales or persons, living or dead, is entirely coinciden-
tal.*

ISBN 0-7414-4725-8

Published by:

INFI∞ITY
PUBLISHING.COM

1094 New DeHaven Street, Suite 100
West Conshohocken, PA 19428-2713
Info@buybooksontheweb.com
www.buybooksontheweb.com
Toll-free (877) BUY BOOK
Local Phone (610) 941-9999
Fax (610) 941-9959

Printed in the United States of America

Printed on Recycled Paper

Published May 2008

In Appreciation

With a grateful heart, I acknowledge the help and encouragement of my friends, Jack, Gene, and Jessica. Gene and Jessica boosted my ego with compliments that spurred me on. Jack showed an interest from the start and voluntarily performed the initial editing chore. (The manuscript has been revised many times since Jack's initial editing, so any remaining errors should not be attributed to him.)

Others have boosted my efforts and gave me cause to continue. My daughter Brenda gave useful suggestions to improve readability of the material.

My father-in-law Dominic and his wife Naomi helped get me started in the store business. This enabled me to become acquainted with the sharecroppers who frequented my store. I shall always be indebted to Dominic and Naomi.

The characters in the book are fictitious composites of the many good people I have been privileged to know and admire. I am deeply indebted to those persons who let me look into their lives and share in their joys and their sorrows.

I am grateful for my parents who taught me that everyone has worth regardless of ethnicity, and that everyone has a story to tell.

I shall always be grateful for the help and support my late wife Juanita gave me. She was a beauty, and for sixty four years she made my life interesting and enjoyable. I'm sure that her vivacious and loving outlook on life rubbed off on me thereby giving me the inclination to put down on paper the achievements of others.

Introduction

Eagle Nest Bayou is an account of what it was like living on a Mississippi Delta plantation almost a century ago. The author operated a general store in a small Mississippi town that served sharecroppers and tenant farmers in the area. All of the customers were honest, hard-working people who struggled to survive when times were hard. .

The fictitious Eagle Nest Bayou Plantation is an exception to what most of the plantations were in that day and time. It was owned and operated by a indulgent old man known as Ole Governor. The story's principal character, Walter Troupe, is depicted as a simple man of solid character of sometimes not so noble aspirations and beliefs. He is composite of many of the sharecropper friends who traded at the author's general store and told of their griefs and joys on rainy days while sitting around a pot-bellied stove talking about life on the early plantations.

Ole Governor is a complete fabrication based on what the author saw as a sensible plantation owner should be. A loner and a self-styled philosopher, he dispensed his views on life whenever he found opportunity. Willie Washington is a man of staunch character rivaling that of Walter Troupe. He raised a family of upstanding citizens who prospered in the world around them. His daughter, Missy Lou, ran away and joined a tent show troupe which devastated her father. Toby Childers was a no-gooder the likes of which are to be found in any community. In that era, mentally afflicted persons were looked upon as freaks, as was Vanessa, Ole Governor's first wife.

Voodoo practitioners were real and affected the thinking of much of the community.

Not one of the author's many customers did all the things attributed to them in the story. These things could have happened, and some of them likely did happen, although no one ever finished relating them on the many rainy-day conversations that took place.

Chapter 1

My Name Is Walter Troupe

My name is Walter Troupe. Leastwise that's what Ole Governor told me it was. He claimed to have saved me out of a house fire on his plantation when I was five years old. He didn't rightly raise me in his own house, but you can say he kinda looked after me after that. I got called his Very Special African, and I had the run of the plantation when I was growing up. It is better to be called an African than some of the things those old white trash call people like us. Anyway, I never minded it. Besides, Ole Governor always reminded me that I was a man of African royalty. He said my daddy was a slave that got taken away from the near coast of Africa. He said my daddy claimed to be a king back there. It didn't help my daddy none because he spent his life chopping cotton and saying Yesser and Nosser to the people who thought they owned him. Ole Governor said that he doubted if anybody ever really owned my daddy because my daddy was a Free Spirit whatever that means.

Being Ole Governor's special African hasn't been so bad. Oh, I've had to chop a little cotton every now and then, and I had to say Yesser and Nosser to the whites round about, but Ole Governor made sure I got taken care of without having to take any real abuse.

Maybe I should explain how it is I speak of Mr, Cassias Aristotle Arbuckle as Ole Governor. It is because long ago some of the people around here tried to poke fun of him by calling him Governor. It started when the boys that were with him at the University laughed at him when he told them that one day he would be the governor of Mississippi. He stood a term as an aide to a governor in the state house down in Jackson, but he never made governor like he had told the boys at the University. I can tell you that he doesn't mind me

1

calling him to his face Governor. It's just natural for me to put the Ole in front of it when I'm not speaking directly to him.

Ole Governor, was a kind of free spirit himself. He worked in the State House down at Jackson when he was a young swisher. As soon as he could, he came back and took over the family plantation from his younger brother here at Eagle Nest Bayou. They say his brother had taken up with a Creole woman from Natchez and she stayed with him in the plantation house for a year or two. When she got tired of him, she ran off back to Natchez. After that, the brother got as mean as a snake and treated the tenants something terrible. But Ole Governor straightened things out when he got back here. They say there was a terribly big argument and the younger brother kinda disappeared. They say that if this bayou ever dries up, they're gonna find a skeleton with a plow stock hooked to a chain around its neck in the deepest hole. That ain't likely to be so because if somebody ever got dumped into Eagle Nest Bayou those ten-foot alligators gonna strip it clean in no time. Alligators swallow bones and all so if all that is true, there won't be anything but a plow stock with a chain tied around it. Some of the old folks around here say that it was Ole Governor who did away with his brother just like he did away with his first wife. I've given lots of thought to that and I just can't believe that a man as gentle as Ole Governor could do such a thing. But you never can tell. Even the best of people do bad things when they get riled.

People still talk about the disappearance of his first wife too. I remember the old folks that worked in the kitchen used to talk about how she went crazy and talked to the birds in the bayou like she could understand them. They never said, much about her disappearance except that she walked into the bayou one day and never came back out. If that was so, then you can't blame her disappearance on Ole Governor.

Now when you read this, you might think I am writing it myself. That won't be true because I'm telling my story to my own grandson that went to school. He is writing it down just like I'm telling him. Oh, he might say "I don't have" in place of my "I ain't got" but it all comes out the same. To make sure that it is the way I'm telling it, I let it rest a few days and then I get him to read it back to me. My memory is better than his, so if he wrote it different from what I told him, I'd know it in a minute. Besides, I can read a little, if the words are not too complicated.

If you should be wondering about the name, Eagle Nest Bayou Plantation, it's because the plantation is situated around Eagle Nest Bayou in Coahoma County, Mississippi. It has about two thousand acres of cotton land, that got awarded to Ole Governor Arbuckle by accident, because he took it over when his younger brother disappeared. The bayou is half a mile wide and about a mile long. It got its name from the eagle nests that are in the top of the big cypress tree that sits in a wide pool in the middle of the bayou. The pool is completely surrounded by smaller trees and the kind of brush that grows with its roots in swamp water. The brush makes it hard to get a boat through, and very few folks at Eagle Nest Bayou Plantation have ever gotten close to the tree where the eagle nest sits.

I need to say that here at Eagle Nest Bayou Plantation I've had a good life. I managed to get through my younger years without getting sent down to the State Penitentiary Farm to chop cotton the rest of my life. My later years have been good too. I have a good wife who was my first love, and three lovely children and one grand son who will take care of me in my old age. That's my purpose in having my grandson write this all down. Part of the reason is to leave a record for the ones that will come into the family in years after I'm gone. Another reason is to let folks know that us Africans and the whites can get along and have meaningful relationships with each other.

I kinda worked up a friendship with Ole Governor Arbuckle that has kept me going through my life. When I was a small tyke, he'd let me feel of the stub of the ring finger on his left hand. As I got older, I tried not to notice the missing finger because he never called attention to it himself. I've seen a lot of things in my life.

You might think that an old African like me wouldn't know anything but chopping cotton and saying Yesser and Nosser, but I've had a real full life. Being Ole Governor's special African has put me in a lot of good places, like when I was young, I was a hostler for him on the plantation. Ole Governor had twenty teams of horses and mules that did the farm work and hauled cotton to the river landing over at Friar's Point, and then hauled supplies back to the main house. Whenever it came time to haul the cotton bales to Friars Point on the river, Ole Governor always put me in charge. We'd start out with five or six freight wagons loaded with cotton bales. We could put four bales on a wagon, but if we added another one, the wagon would likely break down in the middle. Now there were times following a heavy rain that the roads would get ankle-deep in mud. The mules did all right, but the horses would balk when the wheels got almost hub-deep. Sometimes we'd have to hitch two teams to a wagon to get it through. Sometimes an old wagon would pull apart and we'd have to pull out the broken sections and patch them with bailing wire to keep going. Ole Governor never minded us breaking down a wagon, but he always wanted us to bring in the broken pieces to prove we didn't sell the wagon to the shysters that run the steamboats.

And let me tell you, those river boat people were crooked from the toes to the top of their head. I sometimes wondered if they had to screw their britches on when they get up in the morning. You take the time I hauled six wagons over with four cotton bales on each of them. The boat captain counted the bales and gave me a paper to take back to Ole Governor. "Tell your boss-man we'll get all twenty bales down to New Orleans before Christmas," he told me.

Now I can read just a little bit, but I can figure right smart like. Ole Governor used to buy a bag of gumdrops and parcel them out to me six or eight at a time. He'd put three gumdrops in one of my hands and three in my other hand and ask me how many I had in all. If I stumbled around, he'd tell me to put them all in one hand and count them one at a time. That way I learned that three and three made six. He worked me up to fours and fives and all the way up to tens, but with that many we had to use pebbles or shelled peas or anything else that was handy. That's why I knew that the boat captain was a shyster.

Now you don't get anywhere telling a boat captain on the big river that he is trying to pull a fast one. He would have some of his deck hands offer you a free ride down to New Orleans with a stop over at the next bend where they could get some sport seeing how far a African can swim in the fast current. That's why I had my mule skinners pull back up on the levee to wait for the next boat where the captain can figure as good as I could. It all worked out though because the captain took back the paper and made some more squiggles on it that I recognized as tally marks that counted up to the right number.

When I was a young stripling full of vinegar and the other stuff they talk about, I decided that Eagle Nest Bayou Plantation wasn't big enough for me. I got to talking to some of the deck hands on the steamboats about the big towns up and down the river and I decided I wanted to go and see one. They talked about New Orleans and Vicksburg and how the women there wore ribbons and bows and silk stockings. They say that the Creole women there had slanted eyes and braided hair and could turn a man inside out with just one touch of her hand. Now all that sounded good, but Memphis was the place that I wanted to see. It might have been that all the other places were down river, and Memphis being up-river I figured if I ran away, Ole Governor would think that I lit out down river to New Orleans. I waited my chance and when the boat had a cotton buyer with cash money, I sold Ole Governor's cotton and got money in my pocket that I planned to keep rather than to take it back to Eagle Nest Bayou Plantation.

Selling Ole Governor's cotton was wrong. I knew I was stealing from the man who had been so good to me, but sometimes you just have to follow your ideas or you get stagnated and dry up like an old butter bean hull. Besides Ole Governor told me my daddy was a Free Spirit and Ole Governor claimed to be a Free Spirit himself. He had told me about some of his own antics, and what he used to do when he slipped off up-river before he married Ole Misses. I'm guessing I could worry about paying my debt to Ole Governor whenever the right time came around. Anyway, I took the little sack of gold pieces the cotton-buyer gave me and climbed on the next boat that was headed up river. It was the Cincinnati Queen, and the folks on it didn't seem to notice when I found a place to lounge behind some barrels and boxes piled up on the deck.

There ain't no way to tell you what my feelings were. I was excited all over about being on my way to Memphis with real money in my pocket. I didn't know what I would do when I got there, but it was a quivering feeling to know I was starting out on a life of my own. But when I really stopped to think, I got scared. I got scared all over when I began to think of what I'd tell the Lord about my stealing when that Great Getting-up Morning comes and He opens the big book and runs His finger down the page until he comes down to Walter Troupe. He might not have the money amount just right, but He would sure have the part about me running off and disappointing Ole Governor something terrible. The Lord might have the part where I decided that since I thought I might out-smart Ole Governor, I might be able to out-smart Him too.

The river boat was slow going against the current that came from the late fall rains. It gave me lots of time to think about what I was doing. Even before it got night time, I was feeling that I was a thief and a run-away. The thoughts of the meeting with the Lord got bigger and bigger in my mind. It seemed like He was sitting on one of the boxes looking square at me.

"Walter Troupe," He said. I didn't know whether to say Yesser or Nosser or whatever. He said, "You got Ole Governor's money in your pocket. I know you been thinking about the things you are going to do in Memphis. I know you been thinking about those highfalutin gamblers that wear those wide brim hats and sport those diamond stick pins in their white neckties. I know you been seeing them sit at those card tables with their money spread on out in front of them. Walter Troupe, is that the kind of thing you've been craving to do?"

I couldn't find the words to answer the Lord Almighty that was seeming to look right into my insides where my inmost feelings were. I knew about the Lord and Him being the Son of the Living God. I knew about Him because Miss Molly, she was Ole Governor's sister, used to tell us about Him when she would gather us little ones, colored and white, and give us lessons in what she called Bible School. She told us that He was perfect without sin, and how God let Him die on a cross for our sins, and if we believed on Him we could be forgiven for all the bad things we had done. She made sure all of us got baptized to show that we were true believers. I knew all that, and I knew that the Lord was disappointed in me for selling Ole Governors cotton and heading out for Memphis to live a life of partying with the women they talked about that walked up and down on Beale Street up there.

The Lord, was still sitting on that box, or at least He was sitting there in my mind. He seemed to have the same look in His eye like Ole Governor had whenever he caught me in a near lie, or even when I broke something and really didn't mean to do it. They say that some people can't see the Lord like that. They say that only those that have talked with Him and have gotten to know Him well can see Him face to face. But I'll tell you, if you ever get to see the Lord when He looks you in the eye, if you ever sit and have Him ask you What? or Why? you are bound to stop what you are doing and give it some real smart thinking.

The Cincinnati Queen was moving up-river fast like. I don't know how far it was, and how long I sat behind those boxes talking to him. But all sudden like, I decided that the women up in Memphis were not worth me disappointing Ole Governor. I know that he would be mad that I sold his cotton, but I'd rather be back there at Eagle Nest Bayou Plantation asking Ole Governor to let me work out my punishment than to be sitting up there on Beale Street with a high-yellow woman sitting on my lap feeding me fried pork rinds and French wine that don't do as much for you as the white lightening they can get back on the plantation.

Now, right then I got to thinking that it might not be too late for me to turn right around and go back to Eagle Nest Bayou Plantation and give back the money and beg Ole Governor to forgive me. He claimed to be a Born-again Christian, and if he really believed in what the Good Book said, he would forgive me not one but seven times. But then again, if he knew that I would steal and run away one time, he might not ever let me out where I could take his money and run away again. He just might turn me over to the High Sheriff and I'd have to spend the rest of my life chopping cotton and saying Yesser and Nosser to the guards down at the State Penitentiary Farm. Even so, I just about decided to jump off the boat next time it rounded a bend close to the Mississippi side of the river. That's when one of the river boat deck hands spotted me hiding behind the boxes and barrels. He called out to his buddies and they gathered round betting whether I could swim to the Mississippi side or would the current take me to the Arkansas side.

There were not many bets for Mississippi, and none for Arkansas. I decided that maybe the Lord had thought it was time to let me die so He could take me to Heaven with Him. That's when I ran past the grabbing arms of the man in front of me and jumped right into the running current of the big river. When the cold water splashed up in my face and strangled my breathing, I began to think that jumping in the river was the wrong thing to do after all. The practical thing to do then was to start pulling over toward the nearest bank. I couldn't tell if it was Mississippi or Arkansas. I really didn't care because I didn't want to sink down to the bottom where some of those ten-foot alligators might have slipped out of Eagle Nest Bayou to see what there might be for them in the big river.

8

There seemed to be a weight dragging me down where I couldn't keep my nose up out of the water to get a good breath of air. It was the gold pieces that I got when I sold Ole Governor's cotton back at the Friar's Point dock. Back there, when I first saw the shining round pieces lying on the barrel top all bright and gleaming in the sunlight, I thought they were the most beautiful things I had seen ever in this world. I could think of all the things they could do for me and how I could start a brand new life as a river-boat gambler, or ever a cotton merchant up in Memphis. Now I began to realize that the gold pieces were what was pulling me down so I reached in my pocket to throw them out and lighten my weight. Then I remembered that if I ever got back to Eagle Nest Bayou Plantation I wouldn't have any gold pieces to hand over to Ole Governor. But then again, I was doing more sinking than I was swimming.

Well, I thought maybe if I reached down and threw away half the gold pieces that were weighing me down I might be able to hand over half the money I stole, and maybe Ole Governor would let me work out the rest at a dollar a month.

Those gold pieces sure looked shiny when I raised my hand out of the water. I almost put them back in my pocket, but my nose kept sinking in the fast moving current. The gold coins glistened in the sun as I let go of them and they fluttered down in the muddy water. But even half of the stack of gold pieces was not enough to let me swim, so I reached back in and threw the rest away all in one swoop. That's when I started to worry more about what I was going to tell Ole Governor when I walked back to the main house on Eagle Nest Bayou Plantation.

Now they say a man in trouble will turn to praying even if he has never so much as asked the Lord to give him money enough to buy a sack of flour for his young'uns. But praying wasn't new to me. The Lord and me have had many conversations through the hard times of my life. I said out loud, "Lord save me out of this water." Too, I got to worrying so much that I didn't notice that snag that was coming up fast in the current behind me. It was a whole tree that got washed into the river when the current under-cut its roots and it fell into the water limbs and all. There were roots and limbs to grab hold to, and I did some real fine grabbing.

Just like any old bottle that you throw in a creek that's bound to get washed up on the bank sooner or later, that old snag lodged itself on the Mississippi bank a pretty good distance upriver from Friars Point landing.

I was one dead-tired mule driver, too tired to walk the twelve miles back home to Eagle Nest Bayou Plantation. All I felt like doing was to sprawl out on the river bank and rest. I must have gone to sleep because the morning sun was shining into my eyes when I woke up. But all in all, the Lord was looking after me. He let me catch a ride on one of the freight wagons hauling flour and salt from the dock back to the main farm house.

All the way home I tried to work up some story in my mind that Old Governor would believe. There wasn't anybody that saw me sell the cotton to the cotton merchant, and I thought that nobody knew I started up river with that sack of gold pieces in my pocket.

Everybody knows how crooked those river-boat people are. I figured that I might just tell Ole Governor that I got kidnapped and they took all his cotton and me along with it down river toward New Orleans. Besides, my arm was bruised with a long purple color that showed even through my dark skin. I could make up a good story as how I wrestled with river pirates and finally got away. I could tell ole Governor that there wasn't any way I could swim the river with twenty-four bales of cotton tied to my belt so I let them have the cotton and saved myself from a life of drudgery on the docks of New Orleans.

Ole Governor acted like he was glad to see me. He took me into the kitchen of the main house and had Esse-Mae put warm wet cloths on my bruised arm. He kept rubbing the stub of his finger and looking at me kinda strange like he was waiting for me to tell him what had happened to his twenty-four bales of cotton. Now I don't think is sacrilegious, least wise I hope it isn't if I liken Ole Governor to the

Lord Himself, but it was like when I was on the river boat hiding behind the boxes and barrels thinking of having a conversation with the Lord. Each time I thought I was making a point, Ole Governor would stop and turn his head kinda slant-wise like he was peering down the side of his nose when he looked me deep in the eye.

It was just about that time that my knees started to wobbling a little because I was afraid Ole Governor was about to catch me lying. I figured if I kept my britches legs real loose my knees would wobble inside my britches leg and not show. But the bad part of it all was that my pants pocket hung down about where my knee was wobbling. It was one of those times when Old Governor had cocked his head and looked at me slantwise that my knee wobbled against something in my pocket. It kinda went "klink-klink" like gold coins clinking together.

Old Governor stopped what he was saying, and asked me, "What was that noise I hear?"

I knew right off just what it was. At the time when I was swimming in the river and tried to lighten my weight by throwing out the gold coins in my pocket, I must have missed three or four of the coins down in the deepest part of my pocket.

When Ole Governor said again, "What's that noise I hear?" I was reminded of the Bible passage Miss Molly used to read about old King Saul keeping some of the cows he captured after the Lord told him not to keep any of the loot he gained from King Agag. Old Samuel heard a cow lowing and he asked King Saul, "What's that I hear?" Old King Saul knew right then that his goose was cooked. He couldn't fool Samuel, and he couldn't fool the Lord either. That's just the way I felt when Ole Governor asked me, "What's that noise I hear."

He kept looking at me until I reached in my pocket and pulled out the four gold coins. Somehow I could tell that Ole Governor knew all along about my selling his cotton to the buyer on the boat even before I came back home to him. It must have been one of the other hostlers that told him.

"Walter Troupe," Ole Governor said to me,, "I thought I taught you better than that. I thought I taught you that If you are going to be anything, you ought to be it right down to the bottom of your shoes. If you are going to be a thief, you ought to be a full thief. Now it looks like you are just half a thief, and being half anything is worse that being the whole thing. Just tell me now. Why would you sell my cotton and head up the river with the money?"

I didn't rightly have a good answer. I wanted to tell him about how I wanted to be a river-boat gambler with a wide brim hat and diamond stick-pin in my tie. I wanted to tell him that I wanted to see if them high-yellow women up on Beale street could turn a man inside out with just one touch of their hands. I wanted to tell him that I just wanted to be somebody. I just wanted to be somebody.

I knew all along that when Ole Governor looks at you kinda slantwise, he could see what's going on up in your brain, and that was just what was happening. I started out by begging him not to turn me over to the High Sheriff who would put me out on the State Penitentiary Farm where those strange men want to try to make a woman out of every new man that ever gets there. I told Ole Governor that I would work out the money at a-dollar-a-week and pay back all I took. I told him lots of things I don't rightly remember what, but he kept looking at me with his head cocked to the side as if he knew I was a caught chicken about to be plucked and would promise anything to get out of the predicament.

Ole Governor put his finger on my mouth and told me to shut up. "Walter Troupe," he said. "I been knowing that you are a Free Spirit just like I heard them say about your daddy. I been noticing that you listened up when I talked about New Orleans and Memphis and the excitement there was in those river towns. When word got back to me that you sold my cotton and took off up river I wasn't much surprised to hear it. I been knowing that there were cotton buyers on the boats that would try to buy cotton from a wagon boss that was hauling it there for his plantation owner. Those crooked buyers are thieves themselves enticing unknowing mule skinners to sell the cotton at fifty cents on the dollar. When I got word that you sold my cotton, I got the High Sheriff in Clarksdale to send word down to Greenville for the Sheriff there to stop the boat and hold my cotton until I could get a legitimate buyer to take it. You might say I still have my cotton, and the money the crooked cotton buyer paid you is just his loss. But those gold coins you have in your pocket are going to have to be reckoned with. They are not yours, and I can't rightly say they are mine either. I know a good place for them. It's that old church building you go to on Sunday there in Johnstown. It needs a new roof, and some paint on the outside too. That's a good place for you to use those four gold coins. It was the Lord that saved you from the river, and it was a happenstance that you didn't throw all the gold pieces away when you were trying to swim in the Big River to save yourself."

Ole Governor hadn't finished. He cocked his head again and said. "Walter Troupe. I don't want to hear tell of you bragging around about how it was you that paid for the roof and paint job on the church. It would be just as well as if nobody ever knew where the four gold coins came from that got found in the collection plate next Sunday morning."

Chapter 2

Keeping the Peace

Keeping peace on a plantation with as many as forty sharecropper families and two to six children in each family is a big job. There's bound to be a squabble almost every week. Toby Childers was always stretching his cotton rows longer than they should be so that they end up right next to the rows of his neighbor with no room to turn around the mules without breaking down some of the stalks that didn't belong to him. Now that doesn't mean that Toby is trying to mess up his neighbor. It might just mean that he was not thinking and forgot to turn off the planter hopper when he came to the end of his own plot. Once the stalks come up, they look so nice and green on the end of the row it seems shameful to chop them down.

Ole Governor keeps telling all his sharecroppers that they have to be mindful of their neighbors. He told them to leave enough room for a turn-row. For those of you who are city people that might read this, a turn-row is the separation between plots that allows room to turn around the mules so you can start plowing the row next to it. A turn row is also a separation between the other man's crop and yours so he doesn't get mixed up and pick cotton on your plot and put it in your own cotton sack. Some folks believed that Toby Childers was one to sneak over and pick his neighbor's cotton and claim it to be his own.

Ole Governor always took me along when he went to settle squabbles between his sharecroppers. It was because hr knew that everyone respected me I guess. They knew that I was considered to be Ole Governor's special field hand because he saved me out of the house fire when I was just a little stripling. Now that doesn't mean that I am wiser than most people. It might mean that I was contented with my place in life and never felt like I had to horn in on anybody else to be satisfied with what I had. I always trusted in the Lord to make everything right with people. When you have the Lord on your side, you don't have to be suspicious of anybody. Maybe that's the reason I never had a squabble with anybody on Eagle Nest Bayou Plantation.

The times Ole Governor took me along when he went to settle a squabble I'd just stand back and kinda listen, nodding my head when he made a point in his own favor, or kinda frowning when the other people looked like they didn't like what Ole Governor was saying.

Ole Toby Childers was a little squirt, but he always seemed to be wound up real tight like one of those little wind-up toy cars you get at Christmas time. When Ole Governor rode up in his black polished carriage with the black leather straps and gold buckles, Ole Toby kinda bristled up like he wasn't going to like anything Ole Governor was going to tell him.

Now the man that was complaining against old Toby was none other than Willie Washington. I never had much conversation with Willie because he kinda kept to himself. He was a renter that owned his own mules and much of the plows and mule-drawn rolling cultivators that make growing cotton a lot easier than if all you got is a mule and a double-shovel plow. A sharecropper doesn't own anything but a strong back to supply the hand labor for chopping cotton and picking it when the bolls open all white. The plantation owner lets the sharecropper borrow the mules to pull the plows, but he makes a charge out on the big tally book of every bale of hay and every pound of cotton seed that goes to making the crop. A renter is considered to be a large step up from a sharecropper because he rents the owners plot and doesn't have to rely on the owner supplying the mules and the hay and corn to feed them. Willie Washington was that kind of tenant.

Everybody knew that Willie put up with a lot of the shenanigans from Toby Childers like when Toby inched over and borrowed rossen-ears and fresh tomatoes from Willie's garden. Now Toby might have called it borrowing with an aim to make a payback when his own got ready for picking, but Toby didn't really have any sweet corn or tomatoes in his own garden at all. As a matter Toby didn't have anything planted but cotton, and he never had a good stand at that. Some folks said that Toby never had a good crop because he used to draw down ten bags of fertilizer from Ole Governor and sell five of them to the farmer on the next plantation so he would have money to buy white lightning from Wilson Womack who had a moonshine still over on the other side of the bayou.

Toby always came out in the hole when settling-up time would come at the end of the growing season in fall. Ole Governor threatened to throw him off the plantation, but Toby would cry like a baby and tell Ole Governor that there was no way that he could feed his six children during the coming winter. Ole Governor must have had a soft streak in him because he would always let Toby stay on for another year.

But this time Toby Childers wasn't crying like a baby. It was because he had a good stand of cotton since he used all ten bags of fertilizer on his own crop. It was beginning to look like Toby's cotton was just as good as Willie Washington's who had the neighboring stand.

Now it wasn't said, but several people made mention that maybe Toby had done some moonlight hunting and kinda borrowed a few bags of fertilizer like he borrowed sweet corn and tomatoes. Willie Washington kept his extra seed and his fertilizer in a shed behind his tenant house but he kept it under lock and key.

Being a quiet soul himself, Willie Washington wasn't one to yell thief unless he had good evidence of the stealing. It looked to me from the very start that Willie's complaint wasn't about Toby stretching his cotton rows but there was something deeper than just bent over cotton stalks in Willie's complaining.

Toby bristled up when Ole Governor got out of his black polished carriage. "What you got against me now," he said kinda tartly, "You always been picking on me and keeping your books so I can't ever have any money at settle up time."

Now Toby's first statement was mean, and his second statement was a direct accusation about Ole Governor's honesty. It was easy to see that Ole Governor wasn't ready to get into any contest of words just yet. He started out with a big smile that spread all over his face. Even his white mustache turned up on the ends like it wanted to be part of the smile too.

"Toby Childers. We are going to have to have a talk, and it won't do any good if either of us make accusations that we can't back up," Ole Governor was saying, "Willie Washington here says that when you turn around the mules at the end of the cotton row you let them trample on his cotton that's next to you. Looks like you have a good stand of cotton this year. You usually have a straggly crop, yet your cotton is green and lush. That makes me a little suspicious because word has gotten around that you sold four bags of fertilizer to Wilson Womack's neighbor early this spring. I notice that you've been spending lots of time laid out on your front porch like you been drinking white lightning early in the day. Willie Washington here says he missed four bags of fertilizer from the shed behind his house this spring."

Willie Washington spoke up kinda apologetically like: "I said I think I missed four bags. I didn't notice the difference until I started running out of fertilizer before I finished spreading it this year. I went back and counted the empty bags and found I was four short from the thirty you issued me this spring."

I could tell that Willie was a little careful not to accuse Toby outright. It was because word came back from the people in the Sledge community that Toby stabbed one of the men over there in a fight over a gallon of red-eye that the man said Toby stole out of his house. Folks around here have been giving Toby plenty of room since they heard about his mean temper.

I could see that Ole Governor was about to get provoked a bit because Willie told him that Toby stole his fertilizer and now he was not standing up to what he was saying. "Now Willie Washington, let's get your story right. Just this morning you came to me claiming that Toby stole your fertilizer."

Willie kinda backed up a step and started to kinda mumble, "I said I thought he stole, er took, or maybe borrowed four bags from my shed."

Now I been knowing about Willie Washington as long as I can remember. He's the man that has that pretty round-faced big-eyed girl named Missy Lou that's been shooting me glances every once and awhile on Sunday at Johnstown AME Church. He has been a stout believer in the Lord, and he is a big man when it comes to standing alongside the average tenant on Eagle Nest Bayou Plantation. I figure he ought not to be afraid of anybody. I guess he didn't want anything to happen to any member of his family. Besides, he believed the Lord's Commandments when it says "Thou shalt not contend with thy neighbor."

Old Toby spoke up right smart like. "Willie Washington. Everybody knows you keep you stuff like fertilizer in that shed behind your house. And everybody knows you got a Yale padlock on the door and you keep the key in the bib pocket of your overalls except on Sunday and then you keep it in the side coat pocket of that blue serge suit you bought last settlement time from Solomon's Dry Goods Store up in Johnstown."

Ole Governor looked Toby straight in the eye and said. "Toby Childers. Tell me how it is that you know so much about where Willie Washington here keeps his keys."

It didn't matter how Toby knew about the key, because Toby had been bragging how it's so easy to pry off the boards on the back of the shed and bend back the nails so the nailheads still look like they are holding the board in place.

Old Toby kinda laughed and said, "Everybody on Eagle Nest Bayou Plantation knows that Willie Washington here is got more than any other tenant in Coahoma County. They know how much he drops in the church collection plate, and how much he pays for them pretty dresses he gets for his wife and his girls. They watch his every move because he thinks he is so much better than anybody else. He's uppity and thinks everybody else is dirt. That's why everybody else is just waiting for his crop to fail so he'll be taken down like them. There will be a day when some lowlife is gonna sneak up on his back and stick a knife in him, or poison his mules or maybe knock up one of his pretty girls. Mind you, it won't be me because I don't do things like that."

Willie bristled like he was gonna smack Toby right in his big nasty mouth. He seemed to be struggling inside because he had just made a testimony in church last Sunday that a body should not be taken to violence but turn the other cheek just like the scripture said. In a minute or two, he stepped back like he had made up his mind and mumbled something that sounded like he would drop the matter this time and forget about the missing four bags of fertilizer and the trampled down cotton stalks on his side of the plot boundary.

Ole Governor looked relieved. I could tell that he wasn't satisfied with the outcome, but he just didn't want to have a cut-and-shoot fight right there in front of his eyes. When Toby and Willie had walked back toward their own houses, Ole Governor turned to me and remarked that he wouldn't be surprised if Old Toby didn't get his comeuppance before the week was out. He said it in a way that I kinda knew that me being his special field hand, he expected me to have some part in the comeuppance.

Now I won't say that plantation owners in Coahoma County always have somebody to do their dirty work. It is not always the case. Some of them are quick to take a swing at a tenant, or use a gun to make their point. I was remembering the plow share with the chain on it that they say is sunk in the deepest part of Eagle Nest Bayou so I suppose that Ole Governor could handle his own problems. Me being his special field hand, I could tell that he was planting a seed right there.

Needless to say, Old Toby Childers got roughed up pretty bad when he went out to the pump for a bucket of water after dark that same night. He had bruises all over his face and one of his arms got wrenched out of the socket where they had to carry him next day to Doctor Stanton to get it pulled back in place. Some said that it was Willie Washington that did it, but I knew it was not him. It was not me either. I don't do things like that. I wouldn't be surprised if it wasn't that Ole Governor called in that big bruiser off that plantation over at Belen who had been known to rough up anybody for a half-dollar and a drink of moonshine.

Chapter 3

Courting Time

It was early on in my young life that Ole Governor decided it was time for me to start a family. Now I can't say that I hadn't already been thinking about marrying up with a young woman that would raise me some children to take care of me in my old age. But you know how it is, when you are young and seeing the grass turn green and the wild flowers a-blooming in their season without having to do anything but look at them, you just don't think of what it will be like in your old age.

Now there were plenty of young chickens round about, and those poulet-kind were beginning to sidle up to me on church days like they would like to visited in the evenings when it was too late to chop cotton or on Sunday evenings when everybody had time off to lounge and pitch horseshoes or the like. It would be a lie to say that I didn't have a kinda inward feeling that a young poulet chicken would he nice to put your arm around their waist and pull them up close. Of course there were papa-roosters, and then there were mama-hens, that were watching over their little girl chickens to make sure they didn't come up carrying a child when they ought to stay healthy to pick cotton and do home chores. I've heard it been said many times that you can't pick your daily quota of cotton when your stomach is sticking out so far that you can't reach to the bottom of a cotton stalk. Besides Ole Governor's sister had taught us that it wasn't right to mess around about making a family until you had a preacher to tie the knot.

The old folks around Eagle Nest Bayou Plantation say that Ole Governor's first wife was a real beauty. She was an artist that came up from Louisiana in a colony where the French people live, and Ole Governor thought the world of her. He bought her everything she ever asked for, and she was always asking for something new. They said she used to go out to the bayou to paint pictures of the Blue Herons and other birds and critters. Some claimed they saw her at night walking around in the shallow water of the bayou like she was looking for something, or somebody. They said she had a bad temper and would curse Ole Governor something terrible when she didn't get her way. Now Ole Governor is a gentle soul, but they said she used to rile him something awful. Some said she went mad and wandered off somewhere and disappeared. Some of the curious sorts around the Eagle Nest Bayou used to say that she was crazy and Ole Governor got his fill of her and took her out for a boat ride on the bayou where the ten-foot alligators thrash around when they smell anything that could make a meal for them.

The second wife that Ole Governor picked was kind and gentle just like his sister Molly before she died; God rest her soul. She was altogether different from what they say his first wife was. We called her Ole Misses since she seemed to be more like Ole Governor than anyone else could be. But I will always remember Ole Governor's sister Miss Molly.

Miss Molly read to all the kids, black and white when she ran her Bible School in the cool of the morning before the sun got up to high and started everybody to looking for a cool shade. She often told us, "The good book says, 'Thou shall not commit adultery,'"

Now I didn't rightly know what adultery meant back then. But it sounded something terrible to us kids. Now days the folks round about don't pay much attention to it. I guess when you got a big crowd of people like we have on Eagle Nest Bayou Plantation you have to be careful that you don't mess up one family with another. I guess it is a practical thing as much as it is a spiritual one. But Ole Governor was careful to watch out how the young married papas kept their hands off the young married mamas of another family. Of course Ole Governor couldn't watch over everybody all the times. I know there were some children in a family that didn't look like the papa, but looked more like the papa of another family. But these things were scarce, and when Ole Governor heard of some finagling around, he would put the finageler off the plantation as fast as you could spit.

"Walter Troupe." Ole Governor said to me one day. "Have you ever thought of starting a family of your own? You know the Good Lord told Adam and Eve to be fruitful and multiply."

I wanted to tell Ole Governor that if the Lord gave freedom to everybody like the Good Book said, then they could multiply without having to have a family. But then, if that were not so, it would mean that there would be children running around everywhere with no one to claim them to see that they grew up right smart like. I figured that me having a family would be mighty nice if I could get the right woman to be the mama. Now the kind of mama I had in mind would be one that would bake you good biscuits and keep your clothes washed, and would sit out on your front porch with you in the cool of the evening when it was to hot to chop cotton or cut wood.

To be real honest, when Ole Governor asked that question I hadn't given any thought to actually starting a family. Ole Governor kept on rubbing the stub of his ring-finger and telling me how good it would be to have children to coddle and even grandchildren to spoil when you got to the golden years of life. He never told me how he lost the finger, and I never asked him, him being such a proud person and all.

"Walter Troupe," Ole Governor said, "You are a big strong man with a good head on your shoulders, what you need is a stoutly made wife that would bring you up some strapping big boys that could chop your cotton and say Yesser and Nosser to you. Now if you want me to, I'll look around and help you find a likely candidate. If you pick out one I'll even go and try to tell her what a good man you are and how it would be good to have you as a husband."

Now I know Ole Governor was kidding around with me just to see what I would say. I told him right off that when the right time came along, I wouldn't need anybody to speak out for me. Besides there was a little girl that I had my eye on for more than a year that I was waiting for her to get to marrying age. She was a bright-eyed little miss with a round face and big eyes that kinda glistened like the sun coming though a crack in the clouds. She seemed to burst out in a smile whenever she happened to look my way in church. Her papa would nudge her in the ribs every time he caught her looking. I heard him say one time, that she ought to pay more attention to the preacher and less to the errant ones of the congregation. I hadn't done anything that would make anybody think I was errant. I guess he wasn't ready to give up one of his good cotton choppers to work in another man's house just yet.

Now if you are smart like Ole Governor, you kinda know what's going on in and around your plantation. Ole Governor knew all along that Missy Lou Washington was the one I had my eye on. I know he was just testing me out to see what I might say when he told me he could pick me a good wife.

Ole Governor called me a Free Spirit, and he was right. I wasn't ready to give up my idea of leaving the plantation and setting myself up in Memphis as a Beale Street merchant. I even had ideas of rounding myself five or six young girls and going to Memphis to set up one of those houses the preacher preaches against. It was only a foolish idea that didn't stick long with me when I realized that in that Great-Getting-up Morning, I just might have to explain to the Lord how it was me that caused so many people to sin just so I could make a little money. I guess it's the devil that puts ideas into your head like that. Ole Governor says that if you get a bad idea in your head, and you keep it there, and every now and then you pull it out to do some more thinking about it, sooner that you can set a mink trap, the idea will grab your mind and you just caught yourself in a trap that has its anchor chain pegged down in Hell.

Each time Missy Lou Washington looked at me with those big brown eyes, I began to feel a need to get to know her better. I noticed that her mama didn't nudge her at all when she caught Missy Lou looking my way. I figured it might be good for me to speak to the mama, kinda pass the time of day, without anything in particular to say. Now her mama was a educated woman that had come back down to Mississippi after living with her aunt up in Gary Indiana. She had been a school teacher there, and she was teaching her own children at home.

When I began to think that it was about the right time to get to know the Washington family, I decided to visit by and take a store-bought can of peaches as a gift for her mama. It was on a cool Sunday evening after church and I noticed that Missy Lou's mama was casting approving glances in my way. Now that doesn't mean that Amanda Washington was interested in me as a man, it only meant that she was seeing me as a possible good catch for her daughter. What I wasn't thinking about was that Willie and Amanda Washington had three daughters and Missy Lou was the youngest of the three.

I put on my freshly starched pants and my new felt hat I had just bought at Solomon's Dry-Good Store there in Johnstown. It was a warm evening and I was afraid that I would sweat and wilt my new white shirt that Ole Governor gave me some while back. Now I won't tell you, but I was a bit scared that Missy Lou or even her mama might laugh at me for thinking that Missy Lou might be interested in me. When you are scared that you are going to be embarrassed, you can think of a hundred things people might say, and it scares you even more. Being scared is not a shameful thing when you are going up in a fight against a man that's bigger than you. You decide that it is something you have to do and you are ready to take your bops on the head if it comes to that, but going up to a mama or papa to talk about taking away their prize little girl is something else.

I had my can of peaches in the sack that it came in from Jimmy Lee's Grocery Store. It didn't seem right to walk up to somebody's house with a sack that they don't know what's inside. Then again it doesn't look right to walk up with a bare can of peaches in your hand so everybody can see what you are giving as a present. Besides, it doesn't seem right for a big man to give a present to a family for something nobody knows why.

I was bothered something terrible, and I hid the can of peaches behind a cotton stalk along the way, but I got hold of myself and decided that if I bought the can of peaches for Missy Lou's mama, I ought to give it to her. The paper sack was still there beside the turn-row where I dropped it. It was rightly clean, so I put the can of peaches in it again.

Willie Washington was sitting on his front porch looking at a Sears and Roebuck Catalog when I set my foot on the bottom step that led up to the porch. He made out like he hadn't noticed me up to that time. When he looked up, he had a kinda half-smile half-frown on his face. I can't say I was able to rightly read it as good or bad. Willie stood up while I was still on the next to the top step before stepping onto the porch. He looked down at me with that same kind of curious look. Now I'm a big man almost as tall or maybe taller than Willie Washington, but he looked like a giant with me still being on a step below the porch level. If it hadn't been Sunday evening and me in my freshly starched clothes, I just might just have cut and run away to hide in my own house, but I knew if I did I would get my clothes all sweaty and have to pay Ida May Wiggins another quarter to starch and iron them for me again. Willie Washington was the first to speak. "Well Walter Troupe. How have you been? I saw you in church today and I noticed that you were not singing as loud as you usually do," Willie said to me as he let some of the frown die away. He took his time, but he eventually asked me to move up on the porch and sit a spell.

It isn't right to tell a lie right out, but I felt like I had to say something to his comment about me not singing loud. I pointed to the edge of the bayou and said something about the willow fuzz in the air kinda getting a body's throat a little fuzzy to. It didn't sound very convincing, but Willie let it go at that.

Willie pulled up another cane-bottomed straight chair and offered for me to sit down. Even when sitting down, Willie Washington looked like a giant. I know he wasn't any

taller than I was, but I suppose it was be
place calling on a girls mother, when
one who was nudging her when she
I gave some more thought about th
if I asked to see Missy Lou's
would wonder why I wanted to t

"Looks like you have some
me, "I've been wondering w
you took it out of the sack
to pick up the sack and put
Willie was enjoying my er

Now a can of peache   peaches no
matter if you are looking at it up   om a far ways off.
I knew that Willie Washington knew   nat was in the sack,
and Willie Washington knew that I knew he knew.

It's hard to come right out and say something that you
know the person you are talking to knows exactly what you
are going to say. I tried my best to sound manfully, but it
didn't look like I was doing a good job. "I just thought I'd
bring a little gift to Missy Lou." It didn't sound just right so I
added: "To Missy Lou's mama." That didn't sound any
better, so I blurted out "Er, Er,… To Missy Lou's family."

Willie Washington stood up as if he was wanting to
make a point and make it real clear. "Walter Troupe, you are
a good man. You are the type of man I'd like to have marry
one of my girls. Now I think you have your eye on Missy
Lou, but there's one thing you have to know. Missy Lou's
my youngest. She's got two sisters older than she is. I'm
going to have to marry them off first before I can think of
letting my youngest leave home. Besides Missy Lou is not
quite old enough to be marrying up with any man. She's got
a lots more to learn before she could keep a man from
running over her and taking advantage of her good nature."

I started to say that I'd take care of Missy Lou and I
wouldn't let anybody run over her or take advantage of her,
but then I realized Willie Washington was talking about a
husband running over her and taking advantage of her good
nature. It never had come to my mind that a young bride had

to be schooled on how to handle a husband. The man seemed to be overprotective of his youngest girl, and I could understand his feeling when I looked at her. She was still a little thing at that, but I've seen girls marry when they were younger than she was.

It wouldn't be right to say that Willie Washington paraded out his two older girls for me to see. It worked out that way when he called into the house and announced he had a guest that needed to be served. I heard him say: "Katie May, why don't you bring Mr. Troupe one of those biscuits you cooked this morning. Spread some of that fig jam you made on it too? And Ethel Anne, bring one of those crocheted seat cushions out for Mr. Troupe to sit on. These cane-bottom chairs can get real hard on a body's back side sometimes."

The two young ladies came out one at a time with the things their father had talked about. The crocheted cushion was very nice with a large sunflower pattern. Willie Washington pointed out that Ethel Ann drew the pattern herself and did the sewing with store-bought thread she had gotten from Solomon's Dry Good Store. He said with pride showing in his voice: "You ought to see the way she can make a bed, nary a wrinkle, and it's so tight you could thump a quarter on it and the quarter would bounce nearly to the ceiling."

"Very nice," I must have mumbled. but I spent more time looking at Ethel Ann than I did the crocheted cushion Now Ethel Ann was a healthy looking girl with strong arms and legs. I'll have to say that she wouldn't need much schooling in how to keep a man from running over her. She looked like she could wrestle with the best of them and always come out on top if it ever came to that. With Kate, it was another matter. She was trim and kinda dainty, but she had those big eyes like her sister, Missy Lou. She talked in a soft tone, but I noticed that the dog lying at Willie Washington's feet got out of her way when she walked near it like he knew what she would do if she got riled. I was guessing that Kate had a way of getting people out of her way whenever she took a mind to. But her biscuits were light as a feather. I could have eaten them without the fig preserves and still asked for more.

Missy Lou came out too, but she didn't bring anything but her pretty smile. Willie Washington kinda said without really coming out and saying it that she had not learned any of the things that would make her a good wife. Even so, Missy Lou would have been the one I'd have picked if her daddy had not said that she wasn't yet old enough to be picked.

When it comes to picking a life-long mate, I'm thinking a body should give much thought to how they would hold up in the long run. If I was to have to pick one at that time. I'm sure I would have taken Ethel Ann because she seemed like she was strong enough to chop cotton all day and still come in and put a meal on the table. But when I thought more about it, I decided that Katy Mae would be the best one because you can't beat her biscuits.

Ole Governor seemed to know everything that went on around Eagle Nest Bayou Plantation because he looked me up first thing Monday morning and asked me how my bride-picking trip to Willie Washington's house turned out. I told him that I just might have to spend more time over on that side of the plantation before I could get around to picking one of the three girls. "You better get one of them real soon, because I hear that a big man from up at Lulu-Rich that's got a little cotton farm that might be coming down this way to pick somebody to give him some children to help him work his place. He'd be smart if he could latch on to Joe Hankin's widow that's already got three young'uns coming up that will be able to hold a chopping hoe in their hands in a year of two.

I ended up visiting Willie Washington just about every Sunday afternoon. I got to know his girls better each time. Ethel Ann was the oldest one. She tended to lean toward house work, I found out that she had the same biscuit recipe that her sister had. Besides, she was the type of woman you would like to put your arms around on a chilly night. She had a gleam in her eye that said she would know how to make a man feel good whenever she took a notion to.

On the other hand, Katy May seemed to lose some of her quietness when she got to know you. She began to look healthy and robust something like her sister, if you quit noticing her big eyes and started looking at her arms and legs too. Now I don't want to leave the impression that either Ethel Ann or Kate were big and fat. Neither one of them had any extra meat on their bones. It was just the way you look at them. If you really looked them over, you might find it hard to pick one over the other, and Willie Washington had gone without coming out and saying right off that he was going to have to get those two married off before Missy Lou would be available for marrying, and he wanted to start with the oldest one first. Now Miss Molly had told us from the time we were children that a man couldn't have two wives. Ole Governor went so far as to say that one wife is enough for any man, and sometimes that's too many.

If I had it my way, I'd have picked all three of the Washington girls. I'd have Ethel Ann to raise up and school my kids, I'd have Katy to cook the meals and make them all strong, and I'd have Missy Lou to sit and hold my hand and stroke my back in the evenings when I needed real companionship.

When I mouthed off my opinion, Ole Governor put his foot down and said that if I was thinking that way, he guessed I wasn't ready to pick a wife after all. I felt that he ought to know having had two of them. I didn't say anything, but I always wondered if there was any truth to what the old folks were saying about his wife going mad and him doing away with her. They said that when she turned up missing, some of the folks in Clarksdale got suspicious and sent the High Sheriff out to look into it just like when his brother disappeared. They say that both times Ole Governor invited the Sheriff in and fed him fried chicken. It wasn't long, they said, before the County Judge ruled that his first wife was dead and Ole Governor could pick himself another wife. They say that Ole Governor had to wait several months

before the County Judge ruled on his brother's disappearance, but the judge declared him dead and gave Ole
Governor the plantation anyway. I'm glad Ole Governor
picked a gentle woman like Ole Misses. She has been good
to all of us here at Eagle Nest Bayou Plantation.

Chapter 4

Saturday Night in The Delta

Saturday is always a special time in Johnstown. It is when everybody gets all their work done by twelve o'clock mid-day and kinda drift up to the nearest town to do their trading for groceries for the coming week. It is when they buy the canned peaches and other goodies to eat on Sunday evenings after church. Saturday afternoon is also the time when plantation folks gather on the sidewalk outside the stores to tell the news about their families and to just talk. The menfolks get off to themselves and talk about crops and the womenfolks talk about their children, As the night comes on, most of the family people go back to their homes, but some of the men gather at the pool hall store around the corner from the church where there is always white lightning and somebody with a fiddle or guitar. The men spend the rest of the night carousing or sneaking out back with one of the loose women that always seem to be handy.

Now Ole Governor didn't seem to condone that kind of thing. I've heard him say that "Boys will be boys, and that's a shame." As a matter of fact, he didn't condone somebody putting up a liquor still on his place, but sometimes they did where nobody could claim that he knew about it. Ole Governor always enjoyed his toddy after the evening meal was finished. He had a special brand that he had them send down from St. Louis in kegs. I remember that we would pick up a keg every now and then that was sent down by river boat to the Friars Point landing.

Now just about every hostler carried a gimlet. A gimlet is a small cork-screw drill that cuts a small hole in wood. I can't say I ever did it, but some hostlers would drill a hole in the side of a keg and drain out a pint or two on the way back to the plantation. They would whittle a peg that would fit the hole and seal it up hoping that Ole Governor wouldn't notice. They said that the Kentucky whisky was good, but it wouldn't do as much for you as the white lightning you could get from Wilson Womack. Wilson never put kerosene in his whisky but used good cracked corn with pure sugar and a little molasses to give it body. He'd let the mixture sit up in barrels for days on end. It would bubble up putting off a good smell that would carry downwind for a quarter mile or so. The government revenue people used to ride around the plantations until they caught a whiff of the good smell and then kinda home in on it like a fox that got a whiff of the hens in a chicken coop. The revenuers would follow their noses right up to the still. But the sheriff's people never seemed to bother anybody on Eagle Nest Bayou Plantation. It might be because Ole Governor always helped to get elected the right sheriff for the job, and the right sheriff for the job was always somebody who didn't bother looking around at what went on at Eagle Nest Bayou Plantation.

Saturday night was the time for letting off the steam that comes from working out in the sun all week. It was not much different from the way the rough-neck whites did down in Clarksdale. Saturday night was the time when old grudges were settled and when new grudges were worked up. There was seldom a Saturday when somebody didn't get stabbed or bopped on the head with a bottle. Most of the fights took place over a loose woman. That kind of woman seemed to be everywhere there is a bunch of men, and that kind of woman would enjoy being the one that got fought about. She would make up to one man just to make their own man jealous.

Sensible people like Willie Washington would do their business in the town and go on back home to get ready for the Sunday church meeting. It was the lowlifes like Toby Childers that would hang around drinking the cheap whisky that Gary Thompson made over on Madagorda Plantation that would set their bellies on fire to the point where they wanted to pass on some of the pain in their innards to somebody else. I've heard it said by some of the real sports around Johnstown that there wasn't ever any bad whiskey. "It's just that some whiskies are better than others."

Now I'm not one to get mixed up with all that drinking and carousing, and certainly I stayed out of any cut-and-shoot fights. It's hard enough to go through life on Eagle Nest Bayou Plantation without having to nurse cuts and bruises on Monday when you are working out in the hot sun. But I must admit that watching somebody else get bopped on the head is interesting especially if it is somebody like Toby Childers that's got a few bops on the head coming for what he has sneaked around and done during his night time foraging. But Jesse Paxton didn't deserve the beating he was getting from the Walsham twins. They claimed he lied to Alice Johnson about their carousing around over at Sledge. They jumped him from behind with Elijah Walsham grabbing him around the chest and Elisha Walsham getting out his razor like he was going to do some real cutting just below Jesse's ears. Now I didn't know anything about Alice Johnson or Jesse Paxton for that matter, but I couldn't just stand there and let the little runt lose his life with a doubled-up attack from two giant field hands.

Sometimes people look at me and call me a giant of a man, and sometimes they look and wonder how it is that I am able to keep from getting into fights. It's because I'm slow to get riled. Well that was not the day for me to be peaceful. I guess it was that catfish I had at Gilmore's cafe for dinner that day. It tasted alright, but I believe it had been hanging out in front of his cafe in the sun too long after Gilmore got the skin off it and before his wife decided to cook it. When your gut is hurting and you feel all bloated up, you kinda want to hit something or somebody, and I chose to wallop Elisha Walsham right beside his left ear. They said I had a soda pop bottle in my hand, and I guess I did. Anyway the lick put a big gash in Elisha's head and he was laid out on the sidewalk for some time. They called Ole Doctor Stanton, but he was slow as always. You won't find a doctor black or white that is ready to come out on Saturday night to treat brawlers that's been drinking and fighting.

Doctor Stanton bandaged Elisha's head, but the fellow never came to. At least it looked like he was going to be knocked out that way until morning. They put him on a wagon bed and took him to his mama's place. Ole Governor came and got hold of me and told me to go to Friars Point and catch a ferry to Helena Arkansas. "If that Walsham boy dies you are going to be in deep trouble, so you better make yourself scarce around this town for awhile."

I have to tell you that I was plenty scared. Even though I was trying to help out Jesse Paxton to keep him from getting killed, they would put me in the jail and a judge would send me to the Parchman Prison Farm for sure. Ole Governor was right. I needed to get away from the county, but it didn't seem right for me to run away before I learned whether Elisha Walsham would live or die. Even so, there was one big reason why I needed to make myself scarce. Elisha's brother had passed the word around town that whether Elisha lived or died he would see to it that revenge would be in store. He found the bottle I had used on his brother, and he told everybody that it would be his tool to beat my brains out when he caught up with me.

To say that I was afraid of Elijah Walsham would not be just right. I didn't want to get into any more brawls. The Good Lord said to "Turn the other cheek." I wasn't against that except Elijah Walsham would use the bottle against my head and not my cheek. A couple of swings of the bottle against my head might just put me out for good. Ole Governor always told me that I had a soft heart, and I was thinking that it might also apply to my skull as well.

It didn't matter anyway, Pete Fleming, the owner of the place where the Walsham twins did their sharecropping, sent Bart Taylor out to arrest me for the attempted murder of one of his field hands. Bart Taylor was the Town Marshal and he asked me to go with him to see the inside of the town's new jail. It wasn't a jail with bars at all. It was a spare room in the town hall building. He explained that the County Sheriff would come by sometime on Monday to take me to the County jailhouse at Clarksdale. "Attempted murder," he

35

explained, "It ain't no big deal. They will keep you locked up for three or four years and then you can go on with the rest of your life. You might have to pick cotton down at the Parchman Prison Farm, but that's not so bad. What's the difference from picking cotton there or picking it here on Eagle Nest Bayou Plantation?"

I could have told him that Ole Governor was a much better boss than those guards down at Parchman. It wouldn't have mattered much anyway. The Town Marshall wouldn't have listened. All the folks around Johnstown had an idea that Ole Governor was a kind soul until he got riled, and then he could be a mean as they said his brother was before he mysteriously disappeared. With all the talk around here about both his wife and his brother disappearing, I began to wonder about him. It would have bothered me in my heart if I ever learned that Ole Governor killed his first wife, or that he killed his brother just to get control of Eagle Nest Bayou Plantation.

Bart Taylor wanted everybody to think he was a gentle soul too, but he had this leather covered lead ball most people call a blackjack that he could swing like it was a top on a string except the top would not make a dent in the skull like his blackjack. I'd just as soon face Elijah Walsham with his bottle than Bart Taylor with his sap.

Life in the Coahoma County Jail wasn't so bad. They fed us on cornbread and peas for every meal. Even on Sunday morning when most people were eating fresh meat from the store, they only put in a little chunk of side meat with the peas.

Word came to me that Elisha Walsham had recovered and was walking around like anybody else. They said he couldn't remember the fight but had all his other senses without any problems. They said that his brother had lost the bottle he was saving for me too. I guess it would have been alright for me to return to Eagle Nest Bayou Plantation except the County Sheriff kinda forgot why it was he was holding me in jail.

Ole Governor came to the rescue. He came and got me explaining that he needed me to help keep his other tenants in line. He said that word had gotten around that Walter Troupe was a mean man with a soda-pop bottle in his hand. The Sheriff said that he would have to pay for my room and board in the jail. I wanted to tell him that cornbread and peas didn't cost much, but it didn't matter. Ole Governor was glad to see me, I could tell. He didn't wrap his arms around me like I was some long lost friend. Instead, he clapped me on the shoulder and laughed when I told him about the stale cornbread. He grinned and told me, "I'll have my cook make you a pan of good cornbread, and maybe we can find some white beans for you rather than those black-eyed peas you've been eating."

Next time I went to town on Saturday night, I made sure I steered clear of the Walsham twins. It didn't matter anyway, they caught up with Jesse Paxton and cut his throat like they had started to do when I bopped Elisha with a bottle. Bart Taylor arrested them and now they are chopping cotton down at Parchman Prison Farm. Folks say they got sent up for life which is all right by me. I guess it means that I won't be running into them again on Saturday night.

Chapter 5

Ole Misses's Trip to Clarksdale

You know, I've done a lot of talking about things in general and I haven't told you very much about myself. I'm coming up on sixty - nine years here on earth. My mother and my papa got burned up in that house fire I've already told you about. Ole Governor pulled me out of the front room window just barely getting me out before the whole house caved in. I don't remember much about what went on before that time. I guess it was because something like a house fire where you lose both your mama and papa and all your hair gets singed by the flames kinda makes you forget all that you knew before that. Besides, I was just six years old at the time. Ole Governor put me with one family or the other for most of my early years. Later on, he let me sleep in the loft of the carriage shed and let me eat in the kitchen of the big house. I guess that I felt more like Ole Governor's family than anything else.

Now in my sixty years or more I learned much about people and things. I learned how to chop cotton real soon, but I also learned that you can use your head and get out of lots of the hard work. Since Ole Governor took a liking to me, he always put me in a place where I could help him out. That's why he always called me his Special Field Hand. Now trashy people in the town have a word they call us people with black skin, but he never let his words slip and call me anything that wasn't dignified.

Before automobiles came into being, he used to have me drive him around in his polished black buggy with the fringe on the top cover and bright leather straps with brass buckles. All the other field hands on Eagle Nest Bayou Plantation seemed to be jealous of me the way Ole Governor treated me. They used to talk behind my back and say that I was trying to make myself like Ole Governor's people. They called me "uppity" and made funny signs between themselves that they thought I might get riled about. There wasn't any use for me to get riled. It doesn't do any good because you can make yourself miserable thinking about what someone might be saying about you. Ole Governor used to tell me: "Don't worry about what people might think. Most of them don't do a good job of thinking anyway."

I have to admit that I enjoyed driving Ole Governor around in his polished black buggy with all the brass buckles and bright leather straps. He gave me a special wipe rag, one of Ole Misses flannel night shirts that she had decided to throw away. It still had the smell of her perfume, but it was just right for wiping the dust off the buggy. I called it a buggy, but Ole Governor called it a "carriage." He told me the story of Cinderella and how her fairy godmother used a pumpkin to make her a carriage. He said that Cinderella's carriage turned back into a pumpkin when she danced too long at the party. I keep wondering if one day I'm going to walk out to the hostler's shed and find that Ole Governor's carriage has turned back into an eggplant it being black like the eggplants Ole Misses has her garden-man plant in her vegetable garden.

The two white horses that Ole Governor bought to pull his carriage were mischievous to say the least, White Flash especially. That's the one Ole Misses named when the man from Clarksdale brought them out for Ole Governor to see. She called the other one White Angel.

Ole Governor didn't close the deal to buy them until he had me look them over. White Flash took a bite out of my straw hat when I lifted his foreleg up to look at his hoof. It was then that I decided to turn down the deal and tell Ole Governor that maybe he should get two black stallions instead of the white ones, but Ole Misses kinda fell in love with the whites. It didn't really matter much anyway. I figured I could handle a balky horse just like a man handles a balky woman.

When I laughed at Ole Governor calling his buggy a carriage, I was not really right because it was really a carriage like Ole Governor showed me a picture of in the story about Cinderella. It had a front seat for the drivers and a black leather cushioned seat for Ole Governor and his Misses. There was a rack on the very back where you could put your baggage or the groceries that Ole Misses picked up at the Montici's Grocery Store in Clarksdale. Even though Eagle Nest Bayou Plantation was close to the little town of Johnstown, Ole Misses liked to go to Clarksdale for her real buying. The grocery stores in Johnstown, and Solomon's Dry Good Store just didn't have the nice things that Ole Misses wanted for wearing and cooking. I remember we would start out just after breakfast and drive the six miles to Clarksdale getting there at ten o'clock and start back toward Eagle Nest Bayou Plantation around four o'clock so we could get back to the plantation before dark.

Ole Misses was a might younger than Ole Governor and she was a classy looker. Her name was Melanie Wellington before she married Ole Governor several years after his first wife died, er... disappeared. She wore the finest clothes she could get from Goldsmith's Store in Memphis, but she didn't get to Memphis no more than once every two years. When Ole Misses went to Montici's Grocery store she would dress up like she was going to a wedding or a funeral. With her broad-brim hat with the little fringes on the edge of the brim and with her lace petty-coat showing each time she stepped down from the black polished carriage, she caught the eye of everybody around especially the men that hung around outside of Montici's Store. Some of them would whistle, and others just stood and stared. Ole Misses kinda liked the attention she was getting. Ole Governor kinda liked it too because it was showing off his woman like a man would enjoy showing off his fine team of black horses.

Us drivers are careful not to let on they notice anything that goes on when Ole Governor goes to town, and much less what we notice when his misses went to town alone. There were times when Ole Misses went to visit her cousin in

Clarksdale and would stay over the weekend so she could go to the First Baptist Church there. She wanted me to stay in town so she would have her carriage to ride her cousin in while she was there. It wasn't hard for me. I'd put up the horses at Tolar's Livery Stable and I'd sleep on the hay that he kept for the horses. Finding a place to eat was hard because nobody wanted black people like me to come inside their eating places. Ole Misses made arrangements for me to show up at the back door of one of the cafe's in town and they would hand me out a plate of turnip greens or some pot-liquor and cornbread. Sometimes I'd get a pork chop, but most of the time it was just side meat and beans.

Now Ole Misses never said so to me, but she let me know that I wasn't to say anything to Ole Governor about what she did and who she talked to in Clarksdale. I can't say that I really had anything to tell Ole Governor since I didn't see anything myself. On the other hand, there were a few things that were interesting to say the least. You take the time Ole Misses was looking for any information she could get about her folks that lived before her. She called them ancestors, and she knew the name of her grandfather, but she could not go back any further than that. I don't know why it is so important for a body to trace back their folks. A person is who he or she is no matter who was the great-granddaddy or great-grandmother. I'm guessing Ole Misses was trying to connect up with Abraham Lincoln or maybe some great king in a foreign land from a long time ago. Since Ole Misses claimed her family name was Wellington before she married Ole Governor, I'm guessing she wanted to be a part of some big English family that she could brag about when she got around the uptown ladies of Clarksdale. She made several inquiries at the tax office to see if there were any Wellingtons living in the area back when her grandfather was a boy. There wasn't much information. But one young man, a lawyer man named William Brazil, just happened to be in the tax office. He seemed to take a special interest in what Ole Misses was looking for. I have to say he was a fine looking gentleman in waistcoat with ruffles on his shirt cuffs and at the collar that made him look like he was a part owner of Wiley's Men Shop there on Church Street.

It doesn't take a real smart person to see what a body is working up toward I could tell right off that the man was more interested in Ole Misses than he was finding her ancestors. He told her about a family cemetery over near Sherrard that might have some grave markers with names on them that could give Ole Misses a clue about her early family. He offered to take her out there with him to have a look. Now Sherrard is not the best place for a young lady like Ole Misses to be out with a man she has just met and had not had any time to ask people about him.

You know how some people can be, and Ole Misses is one of that type. They want to feel like they are interesting and important in someone else's eyes. They want to kinda play around with the idea that they can tip-toe in mischief and not get any of it on their clean-polished shoes. They think they are smart enough to stay out of anything that is wrong or sinful and still enjoy the game of playing around it. I kinda feel that Ole Misses could see in William Brazil the same thing that I saw. Surely she could tell that he just wanted to get her away from everybody in town and whisper sweet things in he ears until she would give in to anything he wanted. I know that she knew better, but I guess it is a thing with women when they are getting on toward forty-five and find the first wrinkle in their neck in the morning when they first look into the mirror.

Ole Misses did show a streak of good sense when she refused to ride out to Sherrard in William Brazil's buggy but insisted that they take her own carriage instead. William Brazil didn't think kindly about having me go along to drive the carriage, but he seemed to think that a field hand like me was really a nobody that wasn't suppose to see anything, and if an "African" did see something, he would be too much afraid to ever mention it to anybody else.

Well Sherrard was not a far distance from Clarksdale, and certainly not too long to make the drive boring. William Brazil started a spiel that he hoped would gain some special

42

attention from Ole Misses. "Mrs. Arbuckle. Er... May I call you Melanie."

The man snuggled closer and started again. "Melanie. My dear, it must be difficult for you living out on that plantation where there are not any parties of festivities within a day's drive. I'll bet you get lonesome out there by yourself. People say that Old Governor Arbuckle spends more time out talking to his tenants than he does entertaining his wife."

Ole Misses was so busy keeping the wind from blowing up her dress and showing her lace petticoat that she didn't pay that much attention to what he was saying. And I have to say that William Brazil was busy himself trying to see what he could see when the wind gusted, but it didn't stop him from talking. "I know it must be hard for you living in a house where two different people have disappeared under rather mysterious circumstances. I know it must be good to get out and talk to real people for a change."

Old Misses held her peace and didn't say anything, but I could tell she was getting uneasy about the way the conversation was headed.

William Brazil took over like he was the same as Ole Governor. He ordered me around like I was field hand working a row of cotton for him. "Boy. See that road that leads across that field. You take it and try not to hit so may bumps."

Now I could tell that he really didn't mind the bumps because with each jostle of the carriage, he seemed to slip over closer to Ole Misses. She didn't seem to mind, because just like I said, she was enjoying feeling that she was thought to be attractive by a man other than Ole Governor.

There was a little lane that led off the road over to a clump of trees by a small lake. The man told me rather pointedly: "Boy. You take that turnoff and keep your eyes on the road. Keep on going till you come to that place by the lake."

I was beginning to see that Ole Misses was becoming uncomfortable with William Brazil reaching around her waist like he was trying to steady her from all the bumps and jostles the roadway was giving. His reaching around was not so well directed because he was reaching for parts of her that she wasn't ready to let him hold.

"Keep them horses steady, Boy." William Brazil was saying "They look like spirited steeds. Don't let them get nervous." I could see that Ole William Brazil was getting more active with his hands and I could tell Ole Misses had enough.

Now I think I mentioned some time earlier that Ole Misses had named the one horse White Flash, and the other one White Angel. I knew that White Flash had one bad trait. He despised a horsefly landing on his rump. Whenever a horsefly got close to him, he would kick his hoofs and slap with his tail until I drove the horsefly away.

When I decided that Ole Misses was more interested in getting back to the main road than she was having William Brazil admire her trim ankles, I decided that it was time to let White Flash think there was a horsefly about to light on his back. I let the reins touch his rump ever so lightly just so it would feel like a horsefly easing down trying to find a place to sink in it's snout and get a good taste of white-horse blood. That was enough to make the animal kick and slap with his tail. A little more touching with the reins made White Flash decide to run away from the swarm of horseflies that was trying to get a bite of his hide. That white horse took out to running like he thought there was a horse ghost right behind him. White Angle seeing the chance for some good running exercise decided to run along with him. The carriage was following behind bouncing up and down with every bump in the path. Ole Misses was hanging on tight, and William Brazil was jostling around trying to get a good hold of something more solid than Ole Misses waist.

"Boy. Can't you keep them horses from running away. Hear, you move over and let me get up there. If you can't handle them, I know I can." William Brazil was standing up and yelling, while trying to dodge the bushes on the side of the path and still work himself into the front seat of the carriage.

When you work that pair of whites like I had done so many times, you can tell when they are running from being scared, or just running because it felt good to kick up their heels. There was a low limb on a tree up ahead to the side of the carriage where William Brazil was standing up trying to get to the front seat. It was just the height of his shoulder, and Ole White Flash followed my guidance and brushed up against the limb like he was trying to brush a horsefly off his rump. The limb caught William Brazil on the neck and swept him right off the carriage just like a chicken hawk that had made a dive down into the barnyard and swooped a pullet right off the feeder.

Now being a born-again Christian, I'm not supposed to take any joy in seeing another man with trouble or pain, but that limb just about took off William Brazil head. He lost his ten-dollar Stetson in the deal but the welt on his neck got redder and redder as we drove back to Clarksdale. Some say that he will never be able to hold his head up straight again. He wanted to blame me for letting the horses run away, but Ole Misses told everybody as to how it was Walter Troupe that swerved the carriage away from the limb just at the right time to keep it from taking off the man's head like a hand scythe cuts down a stalk of corn.

When Ole Misses got back to Eagle Nest Bayou Plantation, Ole Governor had already heard about William Brazil almost losing his head. I can't say that Ole Misses pulled a deal on Ole Governor when she kinda dressed up the story to keep it from sounding like she wanted to go out with William Brazil. Ole Governor kinda took pride in the fact that his misses was desirable by somebody else. It might have been that he wanted to let her think that she was still a beauty that was worth looking at. I'm kinda thinking that he was giving her a present by letting her have a near affair so long as it didn't stir up the gossipers of Coahoma County.

Chapter 6

Reminiscing

Ole Governor never asked me what went on when he let Ole Misses go to Clarksdale to visit her cousin. I kinda guess that he had gotten word from somebody that the lawyer man made a fool of himself when he tried to take Ole Misses out for a romantic ride looking for a family cemetery. Maybe he knew that Walter Troupe would never let anything happen to his special love.

You never can tell, but Ole Governor seemed to want to talk about man and woman and the way they get along with each other. When we went out riding looking at his corn crop over on the other side of Eagle Nest Bayou, he had me pull over under the shade of a big willow tree on the bank of the bayou. I noticed that when he got out of the carriage, he would walk carefully around one certain spot in the grass of the place he had selected for us to sit. For a long time he stood looking over the bayou like he was deep in thought. Ole Misses might have called it meditation, but I could tell that this certain spot had a deep meaning for him. He finally sat down, and pointed for me to sit down too. He opened the basket of fried chicken Mandy fixed for him for his lunch and said a short Thanks for what the Lord had provided. Ole Mandy always put more in than one man could eat so Ole Governor shared his lunch with me. He didn't mind eating with a man of another color of skin, or at least he didn't mind "breaking bread," -- that's the way he said it -- with the likes of me. Too, Ole Mandy put in a jug of lemonade along with two polished clean glasses from the cupboard in the kitchen.

"You know," Ole Governor started his lecturing speech when he handed me a chicken leg from Mandy's basket. "You know, the Lord made man with an appetite for good food. I'm mighty glad he didn't expect us to eat the 'herb of the field' all our life like he once told Adam and Eve in the garden of Eden. I'm mighty glad he made little chickens that could be killed and eaten all in one setting so you wouldn't feel guilty in having to throw away left-over pieces like you would have to do if it was ham or leg of lamb when you couldn't eat all of before the rest spoiled. You know, a chicken is just right to make a meal for one family, and if you're not ready to eat chicken, then you can fry the eggs and eat them."

Ole Governor thought of himself as a real thinker. He was always giving me little bits of wisdom that he had come up with. I guess that is one of the reasons he liked to have me drive him around Eagle Nest Bayou Plantation. It was easy for him to talk to me, but if it was another man of his own kind, he just might not want to give his advice and little bits of wisdom for fear he might be considered a soft old fool.

He started again. "And you remember how the Lord made Adam and decided he needed a help-mate to get him through life without too many problems." I knew the story of Adam and Eve just as well as he did. I always listened carefully when his sister, Miss Molly, read us the story over and over again. When it came to the part about the serpent fooling Eve with the apple off the tree, we kids couldn't understand how it was that a snake could climb a tree and bring down an apple when he didn't have hands like you and me. But there was one thing we could understand and that was that a snake was evil and was to be looked out for when you are walking around the edge of Eagle Nest Bayou. Those ugly water moccasins would crawl out on the bank and lie there in the sun like us cotton choppers liked to do at mid day when we had eaten our cornbread and side meat. In the early spring when the cotton first comes up, there always seemed to be a cool breeze coming off the bayou. That's when it is good to lie on the soft green grass and let the sun warm your bones. You can look up a the blue sky and wonder what it's going to be like when the Lord calls you home to His Paradise. That's the way a water moccasin must feel the need to do when he crawls out of the water and spreads himself out on the muddy bank of the bayou, except you know that an evil thing like a water moccasin couldn't ever expect to be called up to Heaven by the Almighty God.

A water moccasin is usually black all over except inside its mouth which is white like a cotton boll. But when he crawls out of the muddy bayou waters and spreads himself on the bank, the muddy water dries on his scaly hide and you can't tell much difference from him than the mud he is lying on. He is just lying there ready to take a big bite out of the heel of anybody that walks up and steps close to him. That's why we kids that Miss Molly taught in our early morning Bible School could know why the serpent, or snake as we understood it, was considered to be the same as Old Nick himself.

But that's not what Ole Governor really had on his mind. He kept looking at me kinda sideways and twisting the ends of his white cow-horn mustache just like he wanted to talk to me about something important. "Walter Troupe. When do you think it will be time for you to take a woman into your house to bake your biscuits and wash your clothes? You are getting on past twenty years old, and most men that old are usually working on their second bride."

Now I didn't know what he was meaning when he said that because I know Miss Molly made it real clear to us kids in her Bible-School class that a man couldn't have but one wife. Miss Molly had passed away several years earlier, but I will always remember her sweet smile and her soft words as she taught us in her Bible School.

Ole Governor kinda laughed like he knew that I was thinking that a man couldn't have two wives, and he explained what he meant. "What I'm saying is that most men have already kinda used up the first wife by making her work hard in the fields and then work the rest of the night cooking his meals and bringing him coffee to drink out on the front porch before bedtime. If she hasn't expired from fatigue, she has likely gotten enough of the man's shenanigans and run off back home to her mother."

I could always tell when Ole Governor was wanting to josh me about not getting married up with any woman till now. "I been noticing that you've been spending about every Sunday afternoon over at Willie Washington's house. I know that he has three marrying-age daughters that don't have husbands yet. I kinda figured that you were over there kinda testing them out to see which one you would pick in the long run."

Ole Governor gets a wicked gleam in his eye every time he starts in to jesting me. "Now if I were you, I'd pick that big healthy looking one. She looks like she'd hold up well on a cotton row or in the kitchen." He ducked his head and added, "or in the bed as well."

Now I've jested around with Ole Governor about things like that whenever it came up in a conversation, but it didn't seem right to jest when we were talking about a woman that would eventually be my wife. And too. I still hadn't given up on the big-eyed round-faced little one named Missy Lou. But it didn't look like Willie Washington was going to let her go before he got the older ones married off.

Ole Governor let the conversation drift away from the Washington girls, but he wasn't ready to give up on talking about women in general. "A woman is a curious thing," he said. "When God made Eve by taking out one of Adam's rib bones, it went to show that He had a sense of humor. He could have taken an ear, or one of the arm-bones. He could have even taken part of a head bone. If he had taken any part of the head, all the women in the world would claim that it is their part to take over and lead the man. Lord knows, they are always trying to do that to us already."

I had to just nod my head. The fried chicken was good and it made me recognize that if I had a wife, she could cook fried chicken just like Mandy in Ole Governor's kitchen. It wouldn't be right for me to try to add to what Ole Governor was saying so I was content to just sit and listen.

"You know, Walter Troupe," Ole Governor kept up the conversation. "Women are curious things. Every time I think I have them figured out, I find I don't know the half about them. You take Ole Misses and the way she took after that lawyer man in Clarksdale. Oh I forgot to tell you. She gave me a full report of how he acted and tried to seduce her out by the Sherrard Cemetery. She really didn't have to tell me. I know, and she knew, that you wouldn't be a tattle-tale about it. I'm thinking that she was kinda proud that another man found her attractive enough to want to get her out to himself. She is a good woman, and I know she wouldn't be untrue or do anything to deceive me. I don't know how far that William Brazil would have tried to go if you hadn't caused the horses to get skittish and run away with that Lothario barely hanging on to the edge of the carriage. I really felt sorry for him later on because he is always going to have to walk around with that crook in his neck for the rest of his life. I keep wondering how he might have tried to explain his injury to his wife when he got home that night, but I have to say again, your Ole Misses is a good woman. I'm thinking that she would have given that man a firm slap on the face if he had suggested something he should not have." Ole Governor really felt like talking, and he kept right on about his wife. "I know, Walter Troupe, that you are thinking that she might have let him think something that wasn't true, that she would have been afraid that you might run back to me with a tale of how she deceived me. You think she was thinking that you were more loyal to me than you would be to her and would come back and be a talebearer. But I know you better than that. I know that you would be as loyal to her as you would be to me. Come to think about it, maybe lots more went on that you are being secretive about because you love your Ole Misses as much as you think good of me." Ole Governor couldn't help but give me a wide grin when he said that.

We finished off the fried chicken and threw the leftovers in the bushes next to the bayou waters. "We all need to feed God's little creatures like my first wife did. Lord knows, it's hard enough for a squirrel or a muskrat to find food now days as it is for us planters to cope with the boll weevil that seems to be coming into the Mississippi Delta area."

Chapter 7

Ole Brutus

There were all sorts of fish in Eagle Nest Bayou. When the rain stops, the water gets murky and after a while again it gets clear so you can see the end of your paddle if you don't stick it in too deep. When you are digging in Ole Misses's vegetable garden you just might turn over a worm or two. It's hard not to quit digging and pick up your fishing pole to see if the worms are going to bring up a fish.

Willie Washington had a boat that he let me borrow every once and awhile. He ordered it from a Sears Roebuck Catalog. It wasn't very big, just enough room for him and one of his girls to sit in with fishing poles. It got delivered by Railroad Express down to the railroad siding in the station Mr. Watts runs for the railroad in Johnstown, and Willie Washington had to go there to pick it up. Even though it was a small boat, it was too big for one man to tote back to Eagle Nest Bayou. Willie Washington had to hitch up his team of mules to his cotton wagon to transport it back to his house, and he asked me to go with him to get it.

I've been noticing that he kinda includes me in just about everything he does when his family is concerned. Of course he had Ethel Ann, his oldest girl, to go along in the wagon too. She seemed to enjoy sitting on the same board seat where Willie asked me to sit. Ethel Ann told me she never went fishing in the Eagle Nest Bayou unless a big man like her daddy went along too. She said Ole Brutus didn't mind whether it was a man or a woman that got scared and fell out of the boat when he swished his tail and splashed water all over the place. She said she saw him one time lying out on the bank sunning himself in the bright sunshine. "He was big enough to stretch all across this gravel road if he ever took a mind to cross over from his bayou to Swan Lake," she said.

"Now that's a big gator," her daddy grinned and said as he turned the team into the main road that led to Johnstown. Willie seemed to enjoy hearing his Ethel Ann talk. I know he was hoping that I would get dazzled by her talk and decide she was the one I wanted to pick for a wife.

Well we got the boat back to Willie's house without letting it fall off the wagon, but Ethel Ann kept siding up to me and kept up her chatter all the way home. "One day maybe you can take me fishing out on the bayou. I know I wouldn't be afraid with a big man like you." It made me feel good that she thought I would be able to protect her, but where Ole Brutus is concerned, I'm not sure that anybody could come out on top in a wrestling match with that ten foot alligator. They say his teeth are as sharp as the blade of the butcher knife Jimmy Lee uses to cut side meat down at his store in Johnstown. I don't doubt it because to be that big, that monster had to be around when the Indians used to hunt here long before any of the white settlers moved in. I wouldn't argue with anyone if they said he was one of the animals that Noah let go when the Ark run aground up on Mount Ararat.

I can't say I ever saw Ole Brutus myself, but I heard him splash the water when he flipped his tail one day when I was pulling in a catfish on the bank of Eagle Nest Bayou. It scared me so bad, I let go of my pole and jumped back ten feet. When I remembered he was ten feet long, I jumped back another ten feet just for good measure. But all that was last year, and if Ethel Ann was in the boat with me, I know she wouldn't show any fear because she called me a big man like her daddy.

There had been a lot of talk about baiting a big hook with a baby billy goat and setting it out on a log chain to let Ole Brutus catch himself so we could get shed of the monster in the bayou. There wasn't any doubt that there were several other large alligators in Eagle Nest Bayou, because Ole Brutus couldn't be everywhere the people say they saw him or heard him bellow at night. As a matter of fact, when one alligator begins to bellow, other gators would take up the song and soon it would be like a rumble of thunder all over the bayou, and it wasn't storm thunder because the moon would be out with not a cloud in the sky.

They said Ole Brutus was the biggest one in the bayou, and even Ole Governor didn't deny it. "You better watch out for that monster," he told me one day. "He is one mean reptile. I know because I tangled with him one day when I came back to Eagle Nest Bayou after I spent my time in the State Capitol down at Jackson. I'm the one that gave him the name of Marcus Brutus because that was the man who stabbed Julius Caesar in Rome centuries ago. You see, my brother Julius caused me to tangle with Ole Brutus. Julius had taken up with a Creole woman named Avellana. She wasn't any good for him. Thank God she went back to Louisiana. Julius was running the plantation while I was at the University and he wasn't doing a good job of it. He was mean as a snake, and his wild ravings just about run off all the tenants. The farm was run down with tall weeds and Johnson grass growing where you see cotton rows now."

Ole Governor acted like he didn't want to talk any more about his brother, but he had baited my interest and I kept looking like I wanted to hear more. I could tell that he was still a bit riled up when he thought of his brother. "I hear tell he kinda disappeared one day and nobody ever knew what happened to him," I kinda mumbled like I was thinking out loud.

"Yes-sir-ree," Ole Governor liked that word and said it in almost every conversation. "There's been many a story about what happened to him," Ole Governor acted like the subject was still bothering him and he couldn't keep from talking to me about it.

"Walter Troupe," Ole Governor went on so I didn't interrupt him, "I know you have heard the story about the plow share and the trace chain. I can't deny that one day somebody might find a chain and a plow in the deepest part of the bayou, but I can't say it would be true either. All I know is that my brother and the plow and chain disappeared on the same night he and I had a knock-down and drag-out fight after I went over the plantation books with him. He was selling off part of our farm equipment to the planter over on the other side of the bayou to get spending money to buy liquor. When I accused him, Julius got mad and jumped in the boat that was pulled up to our dock. Some say that the plowshare and the chain were in the boat when he took off in it. All I know is he never came back, and we figure that he got reckless and let Ole Brutus get in the boat with him. I know one thing. If it was that alligator that got him. The gold signet ring that my daddy gave Julius when he bequeathed him all his land holdings ought to still be in the stomach of that alligator. If somebody ever catches Ole Brutus, I'm gonna cut open his belly and retrieve that ring that was rightly mine in the first place along with the rest of the estate. In the end, I got awarded the plantation when the County Judge held a hearing and declared my brother dead and the estate mine."

Ole Governor looked like he just had to keep talking about his brother and the way he disappeared. "Some folks said I had a hand in Julius's disappearance. I've lost sleep over that many a night when the wind howls and those alligators get to bellowing deep in the bayou. I have to say that I got riled at my brother at the way he let the plantation run down, but I really loved him. I'm still bothered something terrible when I think of that night long ago."

I could tell that Ole Governor had a heavy load on him that reached right down to his very soul. I wasn't sure that he was telling me the full story, but that didn't matter. I figured that if he had done away with his brother, he would have to answer to the Lord and not me on that day of judgment I decide that if I lived long enough the whole story would come out. Even so, it hurt me down deep when I had suspicious thoughts about the man who always treated me so good.

Somehow Jody Jensen got word about Ole Governor talking about the gold ring. It got to be a big thing with him because Jody felt that the ring would be worth several hundred dollars on the gold market and that Ole Governor might be willing to give much more than that if we found it and offered it to him. Jody talked about it every time we got together. "If we could get the welding shop in Johnstown to weld up a big fish hook, we could put it on a chain and bait it with one of those goats that roam the woods over at Crenshaw, we just might catch Ole Brutus and get the ring and sell it."

Now I wasn't as much interested in getting the ring as I was in the sporting thing of fishing for an alligator. I was thinking that if we could catch Ole Brutus, everybody in the county would come by to see our catch. No doubt, the people in Clarksdale might want to buy the carcass and stuff it to put up outside Montici's Grocery store to bring in customers to look at it. If that happened, they would have to tell everybody that a field hand over at Eagle Nest Bayou Plantation named Walter Troupe was the one that caught it. With that sort of reputation, maybe Willie Washington would not be so strong on marrying off his oldest, and maybe he would let me have Missy Lou the one I have wanted all the time.

Well our alligator fishing project worked. Ole Brutus took the bait. It was in the middle of the night and we could hear the bellowing and thrashing in the water all over the plantation. At first everybody was afraid to get close to the place where he was thrashing. The commotion went on for most of the morning and toward mid afternoon it eased off. We had the chain anchored to a big Cypress tree on the near bank of the bayou.

I'll have to say that when Ole Brutus was thrashing in the early morning, that whole tree seemed to quiver like it wasn't agreeing with the catching of that wild alligator. I guess all of nature seems to want to protect its own in the world of things that God made that was not made in His own image. I mean by that anything that didn't have a mind and heart for love like the Almighty Himself might want to protect its own kind. On the other hand. it might be the powerful struggling of that monster pulling on the chain anchored to the tree that was shaking it from it's roots up.

In middle of the afternoon, the quivering of the tree seemed to quiet down, and we figured it was time to haul in that ten-foot long alligator. Jody Jensen hitched up one of his mules to the anchor chain and we started pulling in our catch. Sure enough, it was Ole Brutus all right. We could tell it by the big scar that he got the time he came out on the bank and tried to eat up one of Prissy Wright's dogs that was playing too close to the bayou's edge. Prissy took an axe and swung it at the head of Ole Brutus making him let go of her dog. The axe opened a gash in the side of the head and just about put out one of his eyes, but it wasn't enough to keep him from coming out on the bank occasionally to look for dogs or small goats once the wound healed. The gator me and Jody hauled up on the bank had a big scar on its head that matched what Prissy Wright said she made with her axe.

Ole Brutus was a monstrous beast. Miss Molly told us when she was reading to us from the book of Job in the Bible that the Leviathan they talked about was really a giant alligator. I'll vow even Job's Leviathan wasn't as big and as mean as Ole Brutus. Jody stepped off its length and after he made four wide paces he was just about to the end of its tail. Ole Brutus wasn't done for. He made one powerful swish of his tail and knocked Jody head over heels back into the bayou waters.

We stood there a long time just looking there at the alligator feeling good that we were about to put to an end the thing that had scared us as long as we could remember. Ole Brutus was just laying there panting and puffing, but we could tell that he knew he was beaten.

It is not a good thing to look at a man or a thing that was once so very powerful and was now laying there kinda cowering like he knew he was helpless and couldn't do anything about it.

I got Jody to hold his head while I loosened the big hook that was in his jaw. Jody got another big lick when Brutus made one more swish this time with his head and gave his catcher another big bruise. Everybody was yelling for us to take an axe and chop off its head. I looked over at Ole

Governor and I could tell what he was thinking. It was like he was remembering that one day, one of the people who was jealous of the way he rode around in that polished black carriage might be glad to see him get a stroke and have to be hand fed, and hand washed, and have his behind cleaned like you would have tend a new baby. I began to have part of the same sort of feeling too. Even Jody must have had a gut feeling the same way. He pushed Ole Brutus around and pointed his head toward the bayou. Everybody thought he was getting ready to split open its belly and see if Ole Governor's gold ring was inside. Like a thinking boy that picks up a baby bird that has fallen to the ground and puts it back in its nest, Jody gave Ole Brutus another push and the big monster kinda wallowed and slid down the bank and into the bayou waters. Just like he was letting us know that he wasn't done for, he gave one powerful swish of his tail and splashed water all over all the on-lookers who had come to see him die.

That night, Ole Governor came over to my shack and brought one of his bottles of French wine he had been saving since the last night he was in the State Capitol House. He made an eloquent toast to nature in general and to the things that we should be happy to have. One of the thing he mentioned was that old alligators and old governors deserved to be left alone.

"You know, Walter Troupe, It isn't often that you see a plantation owner sitting down in a sharecropper shack and passing the bottle back and forth like there isn't any difference between the two of them but an incident of birth."

I had to agree with him. That was something I had never heard of, but it was a good feeling to be there sharing thoughts and stories with a man that was much higher on the social ladder that I would ever hope to be. I'm guessing that Ole Governor never had anybody that he could talk to about his gut notions without feeling that they would be repeated in a crowd and where everybody would have a big laugh. One of the things that I always did was to never repeat anything that I thought might be embarrassing to a person. Lord knows, we all have enough problems without some busybody trying to make sport of something odd we did or happened to say.

"No Walter Troupe," He said, "the incident of birth is a tall yet a bottomless subject to think about. I got it all figured out, or I got figured out how it could be. I'm guessing that the Lord has got a barrel full of little babies just ready waiting to be born. When it comes time for a woman to give birth, he reaches down and gets one from the barrel and hands it to an angel to take down and give to the woman. Now, I'm thinking that when it came time for my mother to give birth, the Lord reached down and got me, He could have just as well reached down and got the baby that would have been born to Allishandra Troupe, if that would have happened, then I would be you and you would be me. What I'm saying, except for the fact that I was the next one in the barrel, I might have been born to a black sharecropper woman and not a fair lady like my mother." Ole Governor took another swig of the bottle and looked at me like he had made a wise saying that some writer at a later time might record as something to write in a book of philosophy.

I had to agree with him that I might have come close to being the baby that grew up to become a respected soldier, or writer, or a state governor like Cassias Aristotle Arbuckle said he was, the man that was passing the French wine-bottle back and forth with me. It didn't make me feel much better about my black skin, but when you are at peace with the Lord, you don't have to worry about little things, or even big things, that you can't do anything about.

Chapter 8

Mandy Gets Talkative

The next day Ole Governor never made mention of the night before when we got down to personal-like talk. He wanted to go riding out over the plantation, and I knew he would want to stop at that special spot down near the end of the Bayou to just look out and remember about his first wife. He sent me back to the house to get the basket of chicken that the cook was fixing for his lunch. The kitchen helper hadn't brought in the stove wood like he should have, and Mandy had to wait till he brought in an armload. She was all riled up at her helper and looked like she wanted to take out her anger on anybody who was handy. She looked at me, but I only grinned when she started talking. "You been dealing with the Ole Mister Arbuckle so long you are getting to act just like him. He won't let anybody get him riled up because he knows it ain't good for his health. If he didn't get his medicines from Stacker's Drug Store every month, he would keel over and die with a paralysis stroke for sure."

Mandy is a good old soul, and she never let herself get mixed up in any gossip or turning to repeat things she has heard or seen that would not look good on anybody she liked, and Ole Governor was one she liked throughout the forty-some-odd years she had worked for him. She was still letting her feelings bother her about the kitchen boy's laziness, and she still wanted to take out her anger toward somebody.

She just had to talk, and since I was handy she aimed her talk at me. "It was that French girl from Louisiana that put him in the shape with his blood pressure that he has now. That woman was a beauty, and she could twist that man around her finger like she would wrap a strip of bacon around a biscuit. Whenever she got upset with anything, she would rant and rave like something awful. She would slap him in the face and run off down the bayou just to spite him. Her rantings got worse and worse, and he couldn't do anything with her."

Mandy kept a sharp eye out for the kitchen boy because she didn't dare let anybody else hear what she was about to say. "I know that woman had something wrong in her head. She used to say that it pained her something awful, and she would get your Ole Governor to massage her temples. Once he put his hands on her, she would yell out all the louder that he was trying to choke her and do away with her. There wasn't no way he could ever please her. I know she was crazy like so many other people said. Yes the old man had her sent down to the State Sanatorium down at Whitfield, but when he saw how the way they treated the people down there, he went down and brought her back home."

I could tell that Mandy dearly loved the old gentleman that I called Ole Governor because she had to use her apron to wipe the tears out of her eyes when she talked about him. "He just couldn't let the woman he loved be in any pain. He brought her home, and it only got worse. She would run off wading in the bayou. It's a God's wonder that the moccasins out there didn't eat her up. It was that big blue-gray stork-like bird that she always would run to. That was something I never understood. The old man sometimes would say that she talked to that big bird he called a heron, and he believed that the heron talked back to her in a way she could understand."

Mandy looked at me with her eyes stretched wide-open with some of the fear she must have had when the French woman was ranting and raving around her. "Your Ole Governor was afraid of her because she went at him with a butcher knife one time and made a swish at his throat that almost got him."

That's when Mandy quick talking. Maybe she got out all her anger and didn't need to talk any more. She did add that the woman ran off and Ole Governor went after her, but he came back without her. By time, she had the fried chicken basket made and she pushed me out of her kitchen and pointed out toward the black polished carriage so I could deliver the victuals.

Chapter 9

Mister Boll Weevil

Things have been running along very well at Eagle Nest Bayou Plantation, The cotton got planted and grew up tall with lots of pretty pink and bluish blossoms all over the stalk. Whenever Ole Governor had me drive him up to Johnstown to get his medicine from Stacker's Drug Store I heard Ole Governor tell his planter acquaintances year after year that the crop wasn't going to be as good as the year before.

The drug store was where most of the planters in this end of Coahoma County congregated when there wasn't anything to do back on the farm. They all liked to sit around and drink soda pop and agonize over the prospects of a bad crop or a change in the government that might cost them more taxes and give nothing in return. I noticed that Ole Governor seldom spoke out in those discussions, but he didn't mind me being.close by. The fellows around the card table where Pete Fleming and Paul T. Patterson who were playing a card game they called Gin Rummy were jesting each other for not being Democrats, They all thought Herbert Hoover was going to ruin the country with his policy of what they called "Fiscal Responsibility." They said that he was not raising taxes, but the price of cotton wasn't getting any higher, and the mills in the Northeast were buying the long fiber stuff from Egypt and Africa. There was a lot of talk about tariffs, but it didn't sound like anybody knew just what it meant.

Other men there would argue that: "Cotton is cotton, and that everybody is going to need to get a shirt to keep out the cold in winter and to keep the sun from burning their hide when July and August came around." They said that the planter shouldn't worry, because there would always be a market for cotton. Ole Governor wasn't so sure, he was still

62

getting the newspaper that was printed in Jackson, the state capitol. He had read about crop failures in Texas and Louisiana and he wasn't sure that it couldn't happen in Mississippi as well. He didn't stand up and spout off in front of his fellow planters, but he kinda mumbled that they all might be in store for a change of mind in few years.

It was true. Word was coming up from down in the South that a little bug with a long sharp nose was eating on the young cotton bolls just when the cotton blossoms were shedding its petals. The bug would stick in its snout and suck the juice from the young boll. The young boll, they called a square, would dry up and fall off on the ground. When Mr. Boll Weevil got fat and sassy with the juice of the young boll, his snout would grow longer and stronger and he would look for some of the firmer cotton bolls he had missed when they were just coming out. Ether early or late in his feeding, the boll weevil was making a big dent in the farmers cotton crop. Now it might sound like I am an expert on boll weevils and cotton farming, but I'm just repeating some of the things I heard Ole Governor tell the planters that were drinking soda-pop and playing cards at Stacker's Drug Store in Johnstown.

Ole Governor sent me over to Friars Point landing with a piece of paper he wanted me to give to one of the river boat captains that was on his way up to Memphis.

"Ten bags of Calcium Arsenate," the river boat captain read the words out loud and commented that he wasn't sure there was a supplier this side of Marietta Ohio that dealt in that much poison. "He'd need just one spoonful if he was going to do away with his old lady," he said mainly to the deck hands hoping to get a big laugh from them.

It took almost four weeks for the order to be filled and put back on a southbound boat. I hauled the bags of white stuff over from Friars Point and stored them in the big barn where Ole Governor kept the cotton seed and fertilizer.

Spring was coming on and cotton planting time was coming up soon. Ole Governor had a gage he used to know exactly when to plant. It wasn't really a gage you could put your hand on, but more a system, if you want to call it that. You know how the women of the plantation liked to fish in the bayou. You'd see them walking down the turn row carrying a fishing pole over their shoulder and a bucket in their hand. The bucket was used to put their lunch in along with the other things needed for fishing like spare corks and lines. Now this is the part that Ole Governor used to gauge when cotton planting time was right. If the woman got in a good place on the bank and turned the bucket bottom-side up so she could sit on it, it was still too early. But if the woman left the bucket standing upright and spread her bottom on the grass of the bayou bank, then you would know that the ground was warm enough for the seed to sprout and come up into a plant ready for chopping.

Well, all Ole Governor's sharecroppers and renters planted just at the right time, and it seemed that all of them were beginning to have good stands a week or so later. Most of the planters would boast about their good stands when they gathered at Stacker's Drug Store and sit around to drink soda pop and play Gin-Rummy. It takes about eight weeks for the cotton to grow up tall enough to blossom out. I remember Ole Governor used to ask me to drive him in his black polished carriage to the southernmost end of Eagle Nest Bayou Plantation so he could look at Golly Morgan's cotton. Golly was one of Ole Governor's chief renters, and you could always count on him for a good early crop.

Golly Morgan was as proud as punch over what he was able to show Ole Governor. The little plants were in straight little rows looking like little green soldiers all lined up marching toward the end of the property. For those of you that don't know about growing cotton, you put the seed in the ground with an automatic cotton planter pulled by a mule. The planter has a little plow blade that opens a furrow in the soil. A wheel that follows will put the seed in the furrow all in one unending line with another wheel closing the furrow. Now you can guess that if the little cotton stalks were not thinned out, there would be too many in one place and they would crowd each other out from the sunlight making all of them stunted. That is why you have to have cotton choppers to come along and thin them out.

There's a six inch hoe and an eight inch hoe. A greedy farmer might like for his choppers to use the small hoe thinking that he will have more stalks on the row than the farmer that let his choppers use an eight inch hoe. But a cotton stalk grows more than waist high, sometimes as tall as breast-high on a high-breasted woman, and it spreads out almost reaching over to the stalks on the row next to it. When the days get long and when the sun beats down real hot like, that's when the cotton stalk grows fastest. Pretty soon you will see a trace of pink in amongst the green leaves. That's when next day or maybe the next, you will see pink and white blossoms all over the field. The bees will start buzzing and the butterflies will flit around all over the place sipping nectar from the blossoms. Ole Governor says the bees and the butterflies are doing their bit to pollinate the cotton bloom so it will have good seed and long fibers.

Golly Morgan had his whole family out chopping the cotton in the field right next to the bayou. He had a hoe in his hand too and every once and awhile he would make a chop at a blade of grass that had come up with the cotton. Good cotton choppers will clear out the little grass clumps so that the coming-up cotton stalk won't be choked out if the grass grows faster than the cotton plant.

It looked like Golly Morgan would have a good crop. If the rains came at the right time he should get his usual bale-to-the-acre. Ole Governor looked pleased, but he was still worried about the insects and the other things that could ruin a crop. One of the things was a heavy thunder storm with rain and hail that would strip the leaves off the cotton stalks and leave nothing but stems sticking up out of the row. When a sharecropper or even a renter had a crop failure, the owner would suffer because there would be no cotton to sell to repay for the furnish or to repay for the land rental.

There are always things to do when a crop is growing. Mostly it is chopping the cotton rows to thin out the plants, but there is the cultivating, the plowing to keep the soil loose so the moisture can get down to the roots. There is always the grass and weeds to contend with. Ole Governor says that the Lord made the herb of the field just like the Holy Scripture points out in the first part of the Bible. He says that the Lord must not have been a farmer because if he was, he would have made grass so it would only grow in a pasture and not ever reach over to a cotton field. Keeping the grass out of the cotton row has always been a problem for the cotton farmer. You chop it out early when the little cotton stalks are coming up, but it keeps coming back just like a squirrel keeps coming back to the corn crib even if you throw a rock at it every time you see it. You can plow your cotton and cover up the grass blades so they will die down, but they keep coming back. That's why you have to plow your rows several times until the cotton stalks get high enough to shade the row and the middle between the rows so the grass gets tired of trying to make a stand for itself and gives up. That's the time we call "laying-by the crop" to let it finish making. That's the time the people on the cotton farms can lounge around and spend their time fishing or just lying on the front porch and watching the clouds float by.

It was well before lay-by time when the little long snout insects began to show up at the plantation. Ole Governor had kept a sharp eye out for them ever since he got word of last year's crop failures in Louisiana and Texas. First you didn't notice the little bugs, you just noticed the cotton blooms wilting and the squares falling off on the ground. For those who do not understand cotton growing, the square is the bottom of the bloom that grows itself into the cotton boll that eventually turns into the white fiber ball you pick to send to the gin so it can be put into bales to sell to the mills for making cloth. Along about that time, if you had looked over your cotton field, you would have noticed thousands of the little bugs with their long noses crawling over your cotton stalks looking for another square to sink their snouts into.

Just like I said, Ole Governor kept a sharp lookout for the pesky boll weevil. When he first spotted the bugs in big numbers, he had us take the Calcium Arsenate he had bought last winter and get it ready to spread it on the young plants. The white powder that is just as fine as the sifted flour a body would use to make a plate of biscuits. The idea was to spread it on the cotton plant while there was still enough dew to dissolve it into what Ole Governor called a boll-weevil cocktail. There isn't any easy way you can spread the poison. Ole Governor borrowed some Ole Misses's pillow cases and had us put a bucket full of the poison in each one to shake over the plants. He warned all the field hands that the stuff was poison. "It comes from Arsenic, and what do you think all those widows used to get rid of their husbands? It's Arsenic that they got from the drug store, when the druggist is the one that's diddling the woman in the first place. Ya'll cover your face with a towel when you have the wind at your front because you don't want to get that ugly stuff in your mouth. You can get it in your lungs and it will do the same thing as if you sprinkled a spoonful of it on that baked sweet potato that you're saving to have for dinner."

Well we got through the boll weevil poisoning program without losing anybody to poisons, but I had to rush Ole Governor to Clarksdale with two of the Jensen boys that got into a pillow fight using the bed cases like they were feather pillows. They had to pump out their stomachs, but I guess they will be alright in a day or two.

Nevertheless, we got through the first year of the boll weevil scare without a crop failure. I can't say the same for the other planters in this end of Coahoma County. Paul T. ended up with a half bale to the acre, and Billy Howell was lucky to get fifty bales on the three hundred acres he had in cotton.

It was just half way through the growing season that Dr. Milton Daggart showed up in Clarksdale. He came in driving a pair of fine looking horses pulling a wagon with canvass sides that had a bright-colored sign with a picture of a dead boll weevil. It was a good thing to look at and see a boll weevil lying on its back with its feet sticking up in the air like it had been charmed into dying.

Dr. Daggart worked his way through Lyon and finally came to Johnstown on a Saturday morning. He had a drum and a bugle, and it wasn't anytime till he had a crowd standing around waiting for him to speak. It was a short speech. "I can tell that you folks are bothered with boll weevils. They came up from Texas and Louisiana last year. Now why do you think they left Louisiana and The Lone Star State? I can tell you. It was because Doctor Milton Daggart drove them out. When they got a taste of Dr. Daggart's special medicine, they couldn't leave fast enough."

Needless to say, all the sharecroppers, and even the plantation owners, stopped to hear what he had to say. "Now the boll weevil has the same natural drives that a man has. He is always looking for a woman weevil so he can have his joys. What do they use down at Parchman Prison Farm to keep the men from climbing the fence to try to get to women? They feed them Salt Peter."

All the men in the crowd nodded their heads showing that they knew what Salt Peter would do. "Now Folkses. I can tell you that if Mister Boll Weevil does not have a natural urge to mate with Misses Boll Weevil, then they will not have any offspring. What does that mean, it means that Misses Boll Weevil will not lay any eggs to make little boll weevils next year. The bad part about it is that there ain't no way to kill all the boll weevils that are bothering you this year. But the good part about it..." Dr. Daggart smiled and made a toot on his bugle as he pounded his bass drum loud enough to make all the people in Johnstown hear. "The good part about it is that if you use Dr. Daggarts Special Elixir, you won't ever have any boll weevils next year or ever again. The ones that lived through the winter will migrate over to Alabama just like the Texas ones migrated here a year ago when I brought my cure to the Texans.

There were some head shakes showing disbelief, but there were many more nods of agreement. I could see that he had the attention of the farmers gathered there on Main Street in Johnstown. He took a small bottle from his pocket and held it up for everybody to see. "Just three drops of my Magic Weevil Elixir will sterilize all the boar boll weevils in an acre plot. Ten drops will treat two acres, and a spoonful will be sufficient for any sharecropper crop here in Coahoma County."

Jody Jensen spoke out and asked: "How are we going to get the boll weevils to drink the Magic Elixir?"

"Now that's a good question. I'm sure that bright young man is going far in this world." He pointed to Jody who couldn't keep from smiling the same way he did when he help pull Ole Brutus out of Eagle Nest Bayou. "Well here is the way you bait those boar weevils. You take a gallon syrup can. Now I know that there isn't a house in Coahoma County that has not got a syrup can somewhere." Again Dr. Daggart got nods from most of the listeners. "You take a syrup can with a quart of water in it. For you people that don't have a quart measurer in the house, then fill a pint liquor bottle with water and pour it in the bucket two times. Next you put in half cup of molasses and a dash of baking soda. Last of all you measure a teaspoonful of Dr. Daggart's Magic Elixir. Let it sit all day and then as dark comes on, put the can in the very middle of your cotton field. Make sure you don't go out and check the bait at night. The boar weevils are skittish and, you'll scare off all of them making your whole project useless."

I have to say that it sounded reasonable to me even though I didn't have the three dollars the man was asking for a bottle of the stuff. But there were several that reached down in the bib pockets of their overalls and looked like they ready to buy.

"You plantation owners standing over there looking like you don't believe what I'm saying." Dr. Daggart pointed to the group leaning against the posts at Stacker's Drug Store. "I have a special deal for the first planter that wants to get rid of boll weevils on his place. For just ten dollars, I'll sell him enough to treat his place and his brother's place too."

Paul T. Patterson, the biggest planter in Coahoma County behind Ole Governor, looked like he was interested. His neighbor, Quinlon Stewart looked at him to see if he was going to buy a bottle. When Paul T. reached toward his hip pocket to get his fold-up wallet, Quinlon beat him to it and bought the first bottle. Everyone gathered around to see what the stuff looked like. Ole Governor was one of them. He came back saying that it was a light purple liquid that smelled much like grape juice.

It didn't take long for Dr. Daggart to sell out all the bottles he had in his canvass-covered wagon. I had other business in Johnstown, and I noticed that the good doctor went into Stacker's Drug Store before he left town. He came out with a paper sack that he kept wrapped up tight so no one could see what he bought. Later on, I heard Bud Wimbley tell his boss Jack Stacker that he finally got rid of the six bottles of grape juice that had soured during the heat wave last summer.

All this happened about the time that they called The Great Depression. They said some banks failed. That meant that they had most of their money out on loans to the big farmers. When the big farmer couldn't grow enough cotton to pay back the loans, the banks tried to take in the land they owned. Even with that, the banks couldn't find anybody with ready money to buy the acreage they had repossessed.

Ole Governor talked with me about it one night when he was feeling bad because some of his friends were going broke. "You know, Walter Troupe, this whole farming system is one big gamble. It's like a big game of craps. You put down your money, and roll the dice. Now, before the dice stop rolling, they got to go through a drought, or a flood, or an insect infestation like we have here with the boll weevil. If the dice can get through those things without crapping out, they still have to go through the ups and downs of the market place. It's not only the cotton market, but the stock market up in New York as well. I hear tell that John Wilton Thompson over at Marks went out and shot himself when his stock went down the drain."

All I could say was "Yesser" or "Nosser" when Ole Governor was telling me this. Now all I got is a little one-room shack that has a fireplace over at one end. Ole Governor liked to sit in front of the fireplace with me, and sometimes he'd just sit and look at the flames coming off the cordwood like he was hypnotized by the sizzling and the popping when the juices inside the wood got hot and busted out in little blue flames. Most of the time he would just talk. I didn't have to say anything because he was getting the loads of the world off his mind. I used to wonder why he wasn't back at the big house talking to Ole Misses instead of here talking to me. I finally decided that Ole Misses was a hot-blooded woman that had all sorts of needs. When Ole Governor got her satisfied, she would dose off in her beauty sleep and be there the rest of the night. On the other hand, Ole Governor, didn't need much sleep. He would keep me up til almost midnight before he found his hat and climbed back on his horse to go back to the big house.

Just about every time Ole Governor got ready to leave to go back to his house, he would always bring up the thing about getting me a helpmate to cook me biscuits and wash my clothes. I guess I had begun to thinking about that more and more each day. I'd been spending most of my free time over at Willie Washington's place anyway.

"Walter Troupe," Willie Watson used to say. "Since you are over here with not much else to do, why don't you take this axe and chop Amanda up some stove wood for her cookstove. You been eating my biscuits that Ethel Ann's been cooking for you, and you been sitting on that cushion that Kate has crocheted, you may as well make some sort of restitution in return."

Now he had the names of the Washington girls back-ward, but it had come to the point where it looked like I was going to have to work for all the entertainment I was getting over at Willie Washington's, I'd just as well take one of the older girls to my own house I knew that Willie Washington, or Ole Governor for that matter, wasn't going to stand still for that unless I got a preacher to tie the knot.

Chapter 10

The Knot Tied

If you are trying to decide whether or not to get married, there are lots of things you have to take into consideration before you know that it is the right thing to do. First off. You have to decide if you are ready to have somebody telling you what to do, and what not to do. Now, I know that a wife doesn't always just come out and tell you to do this or do that. Oh, some of them do, but you can spot that kind right off and mark them off your list. Women have a way of letting you know what they want. They put it in such a way that you feel real bad if you don't pamper them. It's the ones that have a way of letting you know that they are counting on you to keep groceries on the table and give them a new dress every settlement time. These same ones can ruin your day or make you feel like you are no better than Old Nick himself when you let them down.

I have to say that Ethel Ann was the one I thought of each time I remembered how good it was to have a woman around to grin at you and let you know that they like being around you. Come to think of it, I kinda had Ethel Ann on my mind most of the time when I was out working, or when I was waiting with the black polished carriage for Ole Governor outside Stacker's Drug Store when he went in to buy his medicines.

It was getting on toward lay-by time, and I decided that it was the right time for me to ask Ole Governor for a family size house and to set me up as a regular sharecropper in the coming year. Ole Governor thought it was a good idea, and he agreed to get me a good house to start out my family life. I didn't know what he had in mind, but he called the carpenter out of Johnstown to come in and build me a brand new house with glass windows and a stove pipe chimney for a regular wood cookstove.

Ole Governor liked to josh me every chance he got. He grinned when he said: "I know how good Willie Washington's girls keep house, and I don't think it fair to ask one of them to move into a rickety old shack when they are trying to train up a new husband to their way of thinking."

I'll tell you this. Ethel Ann was getting better looking every time I took the time to look at her good. She was tall and big breasted, and if she stood right in front of me, I could just barely see over the top of her head. You could say that the two of us would make a right smart looking couple. With her being the oldest, Willie Washington would be tickled to marry her off. But that wasn't the way he looked at it.

"Walter Troupe." He said like he was about to bust out with one of his testimonies like he did sometimes in the church at Johnstown. "Walter Troupe. Marrying a woman is a serious thing. In the Washington family, you marry for life. You don't make a trial thing, and give the woman back to the papa like you would if the livery stable sells you a mule that has a lame foot. Besides, you haven't asked Ethel Ann. You might find that she has smiled and joked with you just to be nice to guest in the home. You might find that she would rather wait to see if she could find somebody better than you in another go-around."

It never came to my mind that Ethel Ann would turn me down if I asked her first instead of going to her papa like I did.

It was on Willie Washington's front porch when nobody else was around that I decided to put the question to Ethel Ann. She was sitting in the porch swing with her feet barely touching the floor to push the swing along every now and then. Her hair was brushed back so you could see her eyes real good. Every once and awhile she would hum one of the songs we usually sang at the church, but that didn't keep her from breaking into a smile each time she looked over at me. She had clear white teeth that looked like each one matched the other one much like what Ole King Solomon said about the white sheep on a hill when he talked about his special love. Big eyes was a trait in the Washington family, and I could see that Ethel Ann had eyes much like what I admired in Missy Lou. The more I looked at Ethel Ann, the more I could see that she was a real woman.

I began to forget about Missy Lou and began to realize that Ethel Ann was the one for me. I went over to sit beside her in the porch swing. She didn't seem to mind when I snuggled up close to her side. That's when I decided that I needed a woman to snuggle up close to in the bed on cold nights, and that woman should be Ethel Ann. I began to realize that it didn't take a cold night for it to feel good to snuggle up close to her any time.

Ethel Ann looked at me, and I think I could tell what she wanted "Walter Troupe, do you think it's all right to kiss a girl before you marry her?"

Well that's all that went on that Sunday afternoon because Ethel Ann told me right off that we needed a preacher man before we did anything toward making a family. She didn't know it, but I respected her enough to never defile her before we were properly married.

Ethel Ann wanted to get married after cotton-picking time so we waited until the crops were in. It took that long for Ole Governor to get our new house built. And he handed us the key the day we came back from the church as husband and wife.

With a solemn look in his eyes, he pulled me aside for a quick word. "Walter Troupe," he said. "You are a married man now. I'm gonna miss those dark nights when we used to sit by the fire in your one-room shack and we talked about the world in general. Now that you have a wife, you must give her all your attention."

I have to say that I wasn't thinking about sitting by the fire talking to another man, I had in mind snuggling in the bed with the woman that I loved.

Willie Washington's wife and several of the other married women on the plantation brought in groceries and cakes and candies for our celebration. Ethel Ann's sisters hung around a little longer after all the others had left so they could let her know that they were happy for her. When they left, we didn't come out of the house for the next two days.

Chapter 11

Tragedy

Well I took Miss Ethel Ann Washington as my bride and changed her name to Mrs. Ethel Ann Troupe. I'm sure you know that everybody gets lazy now and then and they take the easy way out of even the easy things. I got lazy and started calling my bride Eth. Now the shortening of her name was not meant to belittle her. It just came natural and Eth didn't seem to mind. It came so natural that even her sisters started using it. Eth's daddy, Willie Washington, still called her by her full name. He made sure that he always put the Washington in front of the Troupe. Ethel Ann Washington Troupe was a full mouthful to say the least. I didn't argue with him. It was much easier to refer to her as "your daughter," when I was talking to him. Sometimes he would frown, and sometimes he would just grin like he knew that I was playing up to him.

Eth was a good wife, full of fun, and always ready for a prank or anything that made life interesting. We went through the first months of married life like two kids playing house together. She was always singing or humming a tune from our church songs. She cooked good meals, and she helped me work my sharecropper plot just like the other women on the plantation in order to get a good settlement in the fall. All the while on those evenings after working in the field, Eth would take down the Holy Bible and read to me. She started teaching me to read as well. I was a slow pupil, but it made me feel good when I could get through a whole Psalm without stumbling over more than four or five of the big words. We stuck to the Psalms because they didn't have many big words, When we got to other parts of the Bible, there were names that even Eth had trouble pronouncing. Names like Methuselah and Melchizedek.

76

Maybe it was because of her cheerful attitude, or maybe it was because she prayed to the Lord for a good crop, but our new crop looked better than most of the other cotton crops on Eagle Nest Bayou plantation. I have to say that our cotton looked as good or better than Willie Washington's crop and he was a very good cotton farmer. We were looking for what should be a good settlement which would make it possible for me to buy my Eth a new kitchen table and a new dress to wear to church meetings.

One evening when I had just come in from a full day in the field, I found her all dressed up like she was going to a church meeting. I played it cool and waited a few minutes before asking what was going on. She let me wait awhile and finally said. "Walter," that's what she called me when she was angry or when she was playing around. "Walter. It looks like you have forgotten something." I know I looked puzzled, but she kept looking at me as if she wanted me to try and remember what it was. "Walter. You promised."

Now I was about to get riled because she was acting so strange, but she had that mischievous look in her eye the same as when she wanted to snuggle up in bed even though it was daytime, but usually when she wanted to snuggle up in bed, she didn't get dressed up in her Saturday go to town clothes like she was tonight.

I guess she felt that she had played her game long enough and she finally said. "Walter. You told me that we would have a marriage anniversary party at the end of six months." Now I was used to people around on Eagle Nest Bayou Plantation acting like old married folks after the first year of marriage, so I guess it did seem a little strange to have a bride expecting a marriage celebration every half year. After she knew that she had me puzzled, she burst out in a pretty laugh and told me that her mama had invited the two of us over to her house to eat fried chicken for supper. Eth didn't expect me to get all dressed up like she was, but I went out to the pump and washed my face and hands and put on a clean shirt so I would not embarrass her in front of her folks.

The fried chicken was good, but I could tell that Willie Washington was still fretting about letting one of his girls leave the house. "I always thought it might have been good if the Lord had given me and Amanda a boy child," he said. The people around the table, especially his three girls all stopped eating and got real silent. Willie noticed this and quickly added, "But He gave three exceptional girls, and I must say, I'm thankful for the three of them. Now. Walter Troupe, I know you can't ever make up for a boy of my own, but you and Ethel Ann Washington Troupe can bring me a grand-baby that wears pants rather than a dress."

Eth kinda grinned, and looked at me. "Can we tell them about something we decided to wait to tell?" I knew just what she was meaning. She meant that even in the early marriage, she was having the feelings of being in a family way, and we decided to wait to tell until she was showing outward signs.

Amanda Washington nodded in a way that I knew she could tell right off when one of her girls was carrying a baby. She was just as pleased as her husband. The other two sisters jumped up on hearing the news and ran to their married sister to laugh and feel around like they could feel the baby Eth was carrying.

This looked like it was going to be the hardest winter season I can ever remember here on Eagle Nest Bayou Plantation. Ole Governor still needed me to ride him around in his black polished carriage. During the growing season he had given me help on my own crop. When it looked like grass would catch up with the cotton stalks in my assigned plot he would get some of his day-labor workers to keep my crop looking good. We poisoned with the Calcium Arsenate and ended up with a fair crop and a good settlement.

With everybody worried about the weevil problem, the planters cut back on the monthly furnish and that meant that there would not be anything left over when the sharecropper went to the grocery store and bought his flour and meal, and lard and syrup.

Jimmy Lee and some of the other stores in Johnstown let us sharecroppers carry a little charge account when there wasn't anything left of the furnish money. Every time I had to get something during the rest of the month to keep groceries on the table for me and Eth, Mr. Lee would remind me that I had to pay off the bill in full when settlement time came. I counted up the months and decided that our baby would come in October or November. All the women folks at Eagle Nest Bayou Plantation kept reminding me that the best time to have a baby is springtime. Don't ever have a baby in late fall of winter. That would be a good time because you can tend the new baby without having to work out in the field, but that will put the new baby in the coldest part of the year. There's colds and croupes and whooping-cough and even pneumonia. That's why so many babies don't ever get through the winter.

Ole Governor just laughed when he heard the women folks say to have your baby in this season or in that season. "Lord forgive them," he would say. "Everybody knows that the Almighty is the one that gives the babies, and he doesn't listen to anybody else's schedule." I had to agree with Ole Governor because things kinda happen, and they are bound to happen between a man and his wife during the first few months of marriage.

I told myself that I would do every thing I could do to keep those ugly diseases the old women were talking about off my baby. It was good that Ole Governor built us a fresh new house that was chinked up real tight. There was a cook stove that would warm up the whole house if I kept it fed with stove wood, and I can tell you that I spent all my spare time cutting stove wood and piling it up against a post just a few steps from my kitchen window. Every once and awhile I noticed that my woodpile was going down faster that I thought it should. Now, I'm not one to jump at conclusions, but I could swear that I couldn't ever remember seeing Toby Childers with an axe in his hand. Nevertheless he always had smoke coming out of his chimney day or night.

I figured that if Toby Childers was sticking his hand in my woodpile on dark nights he wouldn't be able to see where he was reaching. That mink trap I mentioned awhile back was still in my box of stuff. I put it in between two sticks of wood right on top of my woodpile. I had to make sure that Eth knew where it was cause I couldn't afford to have her get her pretty fingers all mangled up in a trap. That same night when Eth and I were coming back from her papa's place we noticed the wood pile kinda scattered around. The mink trap was still tied to the log where I anchored it, but it looked like there was some blood on one of its jaws. Next day we noticed that Toby Childers was walking around with a pillow-case bandage on his hand. It wouldn't have done any good to get into a squabble with Toby. He was suffering from his evil deeds and that was enough for the time being.

Ole Governor knew about the thing with Toby Childers and the mink trap. "You watch out for that rascal," he told me. "It has been Toby Childers that's been dropping a word every now and then about the disappearance of my first wife, and my brother Julius too. Now I am not afraid of what anybody might say about me, and I'm sure not afraid about what some of them might think. It's just bothers me to think every time the subject comes up that somebody might hate me. I have nightmares when I think of the night Vanessa got to raving and I couldn't do anything to get her quieted down. You know how it is when you have a guilt, and like that man Shakespear wrote about Lady Macbeth you are devastated by any thing that looks like an ugly spot."

But anything that bothered Ole Governor couldn't even get close to what happened to me on the night after that. I remember it was on an early October night when Eth began to have pains in her belly. We figured it was too soon for the baby, and that's when I got scared. I ran all the way up to the big house and told Ole Governor that Ethel Ann was ailing. He asked me a few questions like what did she eat for supper, but Ole Misses was more direct with her questions. When she heard me mention that there was a trace of blood on the bed sheet, she got her coat and had me harness up the polished black carriage and drive her over to see what might be the matter.

Ole Misses must have suspected something bad wrong because she told me to go and get Ole Governor and tell him we had to take Ethel Ann to the Clarksdale Hospital. Now the folks at the hospital didn't want to take in a sharecropper woman especially when she wasn't white like the other patients there. That's the first time I ever heard Ole Governor swear, but he told those nurses to get that woman a doctor even if he had to treat her out there in his black polished carriage. "By God, I help buy this blasted hospital with two ten-thousand dollar contributions, and you SOBs better get this woman some medical attention right now." I'm not sure, but I think he was acting that way because I was his favorite among all his field hands and he had taken a liking to me and Ethel Ann being together in a family.

Young Doctor McKewin was the one they rousted out from his sleep to come to see my little Eth. The good doctor jumped all over the night nurses for not having her in a bed in the Emergency end of the hospital. They rushed her in and Doctor McKewin rolled up his sleeves and went to work.

I'm guessing that the long bumpy ride to Clarksdale with my little Eth groaning with each bump made her bleeding get worse. Dr. McKewin couldn't get the bleeding stopped and my dear little Ethel Ann passed on to be with her Heavenly Father before it came daylight.

We wanted to have her buried in Johnstown. The people in charge of the cemetery there wouldn't let us bury her in the main part. They claimed that they had a place for the Coloreds. It was a section over behind the cemetery fence that was all grown up with weeds. "It's in the Old Slave section," Miss Mildred Cagel told us. "Maybe they have a burial place up at the Johnstown colored church," she said.

Ole Governor just about blew his top again like he did at Clarksdale Hospital. "That woman that died is not a slave, and I ain't going to have the wife of my Special Carriage Driver get buried in no Slave Cemetery. If I have to, I'll make a special burial place on my own land for special people to rest in peace."

That's just what he did. He set aside a spot over at the far end of Eagle Nest Bayou and marked it off for a fence to be put up whenever he could get the company over at Clarksdale to do it. It made me feel good that my Ethel Ann was resting on Eagle Nest Bayou Plantation close to me and the remainder of the family.

Chapter 12

The Eagle Nest

All the commotion of getting my Ethel Ann a suitable resting place kept my mind from hurting, but when I saw Jody Jensen's boys shoveling in the last bit of dirt and making a little upturned boat-like mound over where she was buried, I just about lost my mind. Ole Governor saw me all churned up, and he told me to go home and try to get over it. I tried to do what he told me, but when I went into my kitchen, it hit me all over again, I thought I heard Ethel Ann singing. On times before, when I went into my house, I could always hear my Ethel humming a tune or maybe singing the words out loud. There was one we used to sing at church about: *Let The Lower Lights Be Burning*. It had a fitting easy-moving gait with words and a tune that kinda rolled out of your mouth. I know it was only in my mind, but I swear I could still hear her singing even though I knew that she was laying six feet underground out there in the new cemetery at the end of Eagle Nest Bayou.

I don't know why it ran all over me like a squirrel darting back and forth over a cornfield looking for an ear of corn that maybe the farmer might have missed when he gathered in his crop. I stopped in my tracks and threw Ethel Ann's Bible book down on the floor; the one that I carried in my hand throughout the whole funeral service. It was God who made her. And it was God who gave her a happy spirit. And it was God who gave her to me. And it was God who let us look forward to having a baby child. And that same God snuffed out her life even before she had an opportunity to ever enjoy bringing a baby into the world.

"Why?" I yelled out at the top of my voice. "Why did you do it, God?" I grabbed a stove lid from the top of the cook stove and threw it against the wall. I wanted to break something like if I had God in my hands, I could let Him know what it would be like to see the one you loved die and be put into the ground. Years later I realized God had the same thing happen to Him when he let His son Jesus die on the cross.

I slammed the door of my house and ran out to the bayou. I guess I would have run farther, but the water up to my knees made it hard to run. Willie Washington's boat was tied to a stake there on the bank. I jumped into the boat and started paddling. I didn't care where the boat went. The boat bumped into the cypress trees and the cypress knees sticking up above the surface. I just kept going farther into the bayou where the biggest trees were and where the brushy plants were the thickest. I pulled my way through the brush until it kinda opened up. In the deepest part, in the middle of the bayou was where the brush thinned out and the water had formed into little pools as big as Ole Governor's front yard. The pools were all over the place and I kept paddling like I was trying to run away from any memory of my little Ethel Ann. I guess I was trying to run away from the God I had trusted all my life ever since Miss Molly started reading us stories about the Baby Jesus and how He loved us. She used to have us sing "Jesus Loves me, This I know, Because the Bible tells me so." Miss Molly said that Jesus is God, and God is the one who made us, and God is Love." I wondered how God could ever think about love when he took an innocent person like my Ethel Ann and let her die a horrible death by losing all her life's blood.

My boat bumped up against a little hummock in the middle of the biggest clearing in the bayou. I didn't know what I was doing but I climbed out of the boat and kinda crawled or wallowed in the mud until I got up to the only grassy part of the knoll. I don't know how long it was I lay there, feeling sorry for myself for ever believing that God was a God of love. I cursed Him something awful which was never in my nature, but I did it because I was disappointed in myself for ever believing that there was really a God who looked over His children.

I don't know how long I lay there, but I must have been so dead tired with all that which happened that I fell off into a deep sleep. I dreamed that I was running away from a monster that kept nipping at my behind with a pitch fork. Just about that time I heard a loud splash and woke up. The loud splash was Ole Brutus trying to get out of the water and slither up on the cypress knoll where I was lying. He had me cut off from the boat. But that wouldn't matter none, because he was so big, he would have swished his big tail against the side of the boat and that light wooden side would have split wide open like a watermelon that you had dropped on the sidewalk up in Johnstown.

It was just me and Ole Brutus. The nearest help there could ever be was half a mile away through some of the thickest brush and cypress trees you have ever seen. I looked around and all I saw was the deep water of the pool where the cypress hammock was sitting. I knew it would not be wise to try to out-swim Ole Brutus. He was born in the water, and he would duck underneath a body and come up with his wide jaws gripping its middle. I thought of what Ole Governor told me about his brother Julius Caesar Arbuckle and how it was likely that his bones were still in the innards of Ole Brutus.

As I backed away from the snapping alligator I came to a place where I couldn't back up any farther. It was the big cypress tree that was in the middle of the knoll. Even though I had cursed God a few minutes ago, it was in my nature to call on Him whenever I was in a tight place. "God help me!" I called out.

Somehow it made me feel good that I was still recognizing that there must be a helping-hand God after all. It was just at that time that my neck brushed against a limb sticking down off the tree. Now I know what you are going to say that tall cypress trees don't have low lying limbs sticking down to where you can reach them. Maybe they don't, and maybe there isn't any way manna could pop up out of the ground just when the Children of Israel were starving to death in the wilderness, or maybe there isn't any way one man could feed five thousand hungry people with six small loaves of bread and four little fishes. Too Paul got complete blindness when the great light which was really a bolt of lightning struck close to him without it knocking the life out of him. People talk about miracles, and the cypress limb was one for me. I grabbed hold of the limb and swung my feet up just as Ole Brutus made a big snap at my ankle bones. I climbed up on the next limb and just sat there while Ole Brutus crawled around the base of the cypress tree snapping and snarling and sometimes bellowing. I noticed that it was a different kind of bellowing that we used to hear at night when one of the gators would take up the bellow from another one across the bayou. It was a bellowing that came from an angry bull gator that could see its dinner but couldn't climb the tree to get it. It was also the kind of bellowing that told all the other gators in the bayou that there was a meal available almost within reach.

Now alligators are funny feeders. Some say they may not eat a meal for a month or more. Some say they might go six months between meals. Maybe it is because if they get a large animal in their belly it takes a long time to digest. That's why the gators that came up to the cypress knoll could be patient and wait. If they could be thinking like us humans, they might be telling each other that they could hang around for a day or a month until the meal that was hanging up there on a limb would get tired and have to let go.

The limb I was sitting on was lean and it didn't make a comfortable seat to say the least. Nevertheless I hung on because I didn't want to be mangled by an old alligator. I knew it was Ole Brutus because he had only one eye and a big gash scar on its head. It was obvious that he was the head gator in the bayou. He snapped and snarled at the others until they all drifted off one by one. I could see their swirls in the water, and every once and awhile they would splash the water with a big swish of their tails as if they were letting Ole Brutus know that they didn't like him hogging the possible meal he had treed. Soon it was just Ole Brutus and me, and I could see that he wasn't going to give up until I got tired of hanging onto that limb and fell onto the grass of that cypress knoll where he could grab me with his jaws that opened up every once and awhile like he was practicing ahead of time for the time I would fall. I told myself that I might just have to get used to sitting up on that limb because it didn't look like he was ever going to leave. I began to look around to see what I could do to get away. Climbing up higher in the big cypress wouldn't help me any because Ole Brutus was smart enough to know that the tree was the only one on the knoll and there wasn't any way to swing over to another tree.

Now the tree that had the limb I was sitting on was the tallest one in the whole of Eagle Nest Bayou. I could look up and see that this was the one that had the eagle nest from which the bayou got its name. Now I kinda think that there are people who don't understand about eagles and their nests. Eagles are meat eaters,. They are a kind of hawk that hunts for small game like rabbits or other ground-loving varmints, but they catch birds on the fly too. There is a special kind of eagle that feeds on fish during certain seasons. That is why they build their nests in tall trees that grow in cypress brakes and bayous. They put their nests in the tallest trees, and the cypress has limbs at the top that spread out almost like a platform. Their nests are made of sticks and twigs so interwoven that they can hold up a heavy bird with all their young as well. During every new season that comes, the eagles bring more sticks and brush to freshen up the nest. That's why there might be as much as a ton of sticks and twigs that make up the platform up there. The nest gets bigger and wider each year. Some of the nests in the bayou have platforms as big as the front porch on Willie Washington's house. This being the biggest nest in the bayou, I'm guessing that it is as big as Ole Governor's kitchen in his mansion he calls Oak Hall.

If you are wondering why I'm taking time away from my story to explain about eagle nests when I was telling you about Ole Brutus waiting underneath the tree for me to fall into his gaping jaws, it's because I wanted you to know that this was the first time I really had given much thought to eagle nest in general. Ole Governor is always talking about what it takes to make a man think. He has always said that a sacrifice is one of the deepest emotions possible. Ole Governor's sister used to read to us about how God let his Son be killed for all our sins. Miss Molly said that was the greatest sacrifice of all.

If there was ever any sacrifice, it was my Ethel Ann that had her life snuffed out right before my eyes. When I looked down at he big alligator in the water below me, I was so heartbroken about losing my love that I didn't care much about living myself. It looked like it was going to be a contest between me and Ole Brutus. I guess that I was just as much interested in winning the contest with the monster that was bellowing below me as I was giving up and leaving this world. I wasn't quite ready to leave the world just yet because I had cursed God for letting Ethel Ann die, and I didn't want to face Him right now.

Well, I knew that Ole Brutus wasn't going to be satisfied until he had eaten up the man he had treed. I looked up above me and decided that the limbs on the lower part of the tree might be dried and brittle and could break if I tried to climb higher. I decided to stay where I was as long as I could hold on. When I looked up above me I could see the part of the nest that overhung most of the top of the tree. There were sticks that looked like they were picked up from trash piles and the like. I could see a faded blue scrap of cloth that looked like it had been part of a man's shirt. A thought came to my mind that made me think that misses eagle picked up bright colored things to make her home presentable to her new born eagle chicks.

Along about three o'clock in the afternoon, Ole Brutus was still waiting like he was never going to leave. I think his occasional bellowing was mistaken by a lady alligator that happened to be in earshot. Now If you are thinking that I can tell the difference between a boy alligator and a girl alligator, I have to tell you that I can't. But you can look at the way they are acting around each other, and tell that there is a difference.

Miss Alligator worked herself up close to the cypress knoll and just stayed there for a little while. She didn't bellow so much as she just called and purred with a hoarse voice like she was lonely. She moved in a circle until she had gone all the way around the knoll. Some of the oldsters say that girl alligators have a scent like a bitch in heat. It must have been that way because Ole Brutus began to ease off on his bellowing and paddle around without moving too far from where he could still keep his one eye on what he hoped to be his supper. Once the lady alligator could see that she had gotten the attention of Ole Brutus, she just swished her tail in easy strokes moving away to the far end of the pool. Ole Brutus tried to keep his one eye on me and still watch what Miss Alligator was doing. When he starting looking at Miss Alligator more than he was looking at me, I figured that if he followed her I might just get to the boat and get away before he let hunger overcome urge.

The fact that I'm here to tell you about it is proof that I got away without being eaten up by a hungry gator. But surviving was not all that good when I went back to my house and knew that there would be no Ethel Ann there to keep me company.

Chapter 13

Toby Turn About

Getting over my Eth's death was the hardest thing I ever tried to do. I wanted to blame it on somebody, but there was no one to blame. I looked around in my life to see who, if anybody, might have had a grudge against me. I had gotten along with everybody on Eagle Nest Bayou Plantation even Toby Childers. I mentioned this to Ole Governor once, but he didn't seem to want to help me find somebody to blame. "Walter Troupe. You don't have to have anybody to blame for things that happen. Bad things just happen sometimes."

I worked it up in my mind that if I didn't have an enemy to blame maybe it would be somebody who was an enemy of Ethel. But she didn't have any enemies as I could remember. She was kind and considerate of everybody. They all liked her. Then I began to think that it might be that Ethel's daddy was the one who would have somebody that wanted to get back at him. That seemed to be something that I could work on.

If Willie Washington had anybody that wanted to do him dirt, it would be Toby Childers. I began to remember something Toby said when Ole Governor talked to him about trampling down Willie Washington's cotton rows and when we thought he was the one who stole the fertilizer out of Willie Washington's shed. I remember it real well because it sounded something like a curse when he said it.

Willie Washington here is got more than any other tenant in Coahoma County. They know how much he drops in the church collection plate and how much he pays for them pretty dresses he gets for his wife and his girls. They watch his every move because he thinks he is so much better than anybody else. He's uppity and thinks everybody else is dirt. That's why everybody else is just waiting for his crop to fail so he will be taken down like them. Some day, some low-life is gonna sneak up on his back and stick a knife in him. Or poison his mules. Or maybe somebody will knock up one of his pretty girls. Mind you, it won't be me because I don't do things like that.

I thought about it for a long time and decided that Toby Childers might be an enemy, but he couldn't do black magic. He couldn't cause anything to happen to Ethel Ann like a hemorrhaging miscarriage.

That was something I needed to talk to Willie Washington about. After all Ethel Ann was his daughter, and I'm sure he cared as much about her as I did. Well almost as much.

Willie Washington was on his front porch just looking out over the bayou like he was in the depth of despair. Sometimes he would rock back and forth in the cane-bottom straight chair he sat in as if he could ease his mind by the motion of his body. He looked like he didn't want to talk so I kinda eased back off the porch to keep him from getting upset.

"Walter Troupe." He called out to me as I was about to step off the bottom step to the ground "Walter Troupe. You look like you've got something on your mind."

I was glad he kinda woke up from his meditation. It would be good for him, and me too, to talk out what was bothering me.

"Walter Troupe. I've been thinking about what Toby Childers said that day when Ole Governor called him up for trampling down my cotton rows." I had to tell Willie Washington that it was the same thing that had plagued me all morning.

"You know Walter Troupe. Toby Childers is not such a bad sort when you look at what he has been faced with all these years." Willie's comment surprised me down to my shoelaces. I couldn't ever guess that anybody could see any good in Toby Childers, and here was a man that you might say got put a curse on who looked like he was making excuses for him.

"I've known Toby since he was a dirty-nose little boy. He didn't have much training in his early days. His mother was a God-fearing woman, but she died when he was no more than five or six. His daddy was a drunk that used to beg money for another bottle. Toby had to make out the best he could. He used to steal cornbread off the porch shelf that womenfolk put out to cool." Willie Watson seemed to feel sorry for the boy and the man he turned into. I remember Willie Washington used to stand up in Johnstown Church and tell his fellow members that everybody has worth. He would say: "God made everybody, and God didn't make no junk."

There on his front porch, Willie Washington told me that he didn't believe anything Toby Childers might have said that could hurt our Ethel Ann. He said that Toby Childers could no more put a curse on our Ethel Ann than a frog could jump through a barrel bung hole.

"Walter Troupe. Are you a praying man?" He caught me off guard with his question. "Walter Troupe. If you think Toby Childers is evil, if he is really evil, it's because the Devil had gotten hold of his soul. Now we are all here together on Eagle Nest Bayou Plantation. The Lord said we should love one another. If we really believe that, we ought to pray for our brothers and sisters even though we don't like what they do. I've had Toby Childers on my heart ever since he said those bad things in front of you and your Ole Governor. At first I wanted to go over there and beat his brains out. But in the end, I guess I realize that I might have been as evil as he is if I didn't have a sainted mother and a God-fearing daddy who kept me on the right path."

Now I can't say that I'm a praying man except when I am in trouble, and then it's where nobody can hear me. Willie Washington knelt down and motioned for me to do also. "In Jesus's name," he started. "Walter Troupe and I come to you to ask for the salvation of our brother Toby Childers."

I was glad when he included me because I really wanted to have Toby Childers change his ways, but Willie Washington was asking the Lord to give that evil man a place in Heaven the same as me.

It took me some real thinking, but I began to realize that if I believed the Bible, I had to want everybody to be able to walk those golden streets just like I knew I would. It meant that one day when Toby Childers was dead and when I was dead, we would climb the golden stairs together. You know. That wasn't such a bad feeling after all.

Now Willie Washington's talk helped me work out the matter that was bothering me, but Toby Childers was the same old evil man, and unless something caused him to change, he wouldn't get any golden slippers but a fire-poker to help Old Nick stoke the fires down there. It was Willie Washington's further praying that made a difference. "Lord, show us a way to get to Toby Childers so we can tell him about Jesus Christ so he will listen."

Prayers are answered in strange ways. Sometimes there might be more pain before there is soothing relief. It wasn't more than a day or two before we got word that Matilda Childers was ailing with the flu. This was the year when they say thousands of people died with that terrible disease. *Influenza*, the uptown people called it, would start with fever and throwing up and weakness and aching all over. If you couldn't get anything to stay down, you would waste away and die.

I heard Ole Misses say that the body would become dehydrated to the point where it could no longer fight the illness. If you got over the worst of it, you still had to take it easy for a week or two before you could get out and hoe a row of cotton again. When one person in the family gets the flu, you can bet that everybody that comes close to them will come down with it.

When we first heard about Matilda, we were wondering who would take care of her and who would take care of her six children. All her neighbors in Eagle Nest Bayou Plantation said Matilda's family was the first to get the flu because of her uncleanliness. They were saying, "She lets those children run around half-naked outside without enough clothes on to keep warm. They are dirty like fresh dug Irish potatoes. They got dirt caked on them that will take a pot of lye-soap to get them clean. And too, they'll pick up and try to eat anything that looks like it would go in their mouth."

I could see that the neighboring women stood around at a distance talking about how bad the sickness was and saying that somebody should do something about it. I noticed that none of them seemed ready to turn a hand to do anything.

Ole Misses heard about the Childers's family sickness and had me drive her down in the polished black carriage to see what needed to be done. She had a freshly starched dress and white apron on when she got out of the carriage, but when she came out of Matilda's house, she was dirty from the vomit and the dirt she cleaned off all the children. She walked all the way back to Oak Hall to keep from dirtying up the clean carriage. She told me that Amanda Washington was already at Matilda's house with clean towels and chicken broth for those who could eat without throwing up.

Toby Childers had seen the family ailing and he claimed he couldn't stand to be there to see them suffering. He went crying over to Wilson Womack's like a child that had dropped his all-day sucker in the dirt. He begged a bottle of lightning, and Wilson gave it to him to get him out of his house. Toby ended up under a willow tree on the banks of the bayou within eyeshot of his house. Every time Amanda or Ole Misses went in and came out of the house, he would say in a slurring voice: "I shore thank you ladies, I shore thank you ladies for coming to the aid of a helpless man like me."

It was hard for me to believe, but Willie Washington's wife, and Ole Governor's wife nursed the Childers's family for five days straight and finally got all of them where they could eat and move around. With her own two hands, Amanda Washington cleaned and scrubbed the Childers's house like it was her own. She threw out and burned anything that was too dirty to clean. But she paid the price for it.

I'm guessing that it was from tiredness, or what the doctors call fatigue, more than anything, but Amanda Washington came down with the worst case of flu anybody had seen. She lay in bed for three weeks with no strength to move except to sip chicken broth whenever her stomach did not rebel and throw it up. Ole Misses was there every day trying to get her to take food.

When Amanda got well enough to sit up in the bed, Matilda Childers came over to help. It's the first time I have ever seen her wearing a clean dress and with her hair combed.

Toby Childers came over too. He was sober for the first time since the flu hit his family. He had cleaned up his clothes too. I couldn't believe my eyes when I saw him out bending over a scrub board to wash his dirty overalls. He wanted to cut wood or rake up weeds from the yard or do anything in the Washington yard that might show his remorse.

It took Willie Washington several days before he would let Toby Childers enter his yard. I heard him call out to the man: "Amanda is lying there sick because she spent her whole self nursing you family, and the whole time, you were lying out there on the porch drunk without helping. I don't want you anywhere close to my house." It didn't sound like the same Willie Washington who only a week or two earlier had told me I should be a brother to Toby.

I heard Ole Misses say that the influenza got into Amanda Washington's lungs. "It had scarred them so badly that she will never be the vibrant handsome woman she once was."

Things happen in strange ways. I was there visiting Amanda when Toby Childers knocked on Willie Washington's front door. His wife Matilda was standing with him looking proud that she was standing by her husband who was clean and neat for the first time she could remember. Toby was holding a green drinking glass, the kind you get out of an oatmeal box and asked if he could give it to Mrs. Amanda Washington as a gift for helping his family when they were sick. I'm guessing the green drinking glass was the only thing of any value he had in his house.

Willie Washington met them at the door but wouldn't let them in. I guess he had forgotten what he had told me about being brothers with all of God's creation. He ordered them to leave, but Amanda hobbled to the door, pushed her husband aside and asked Toby and Matilda to come in.

Toby begged forgiveness for what he had done or what he had failed to do. He wanted to join in on the feeling that made Amanda Washington give her time and now her health to help make his family well. "Whatever the thing she has, I want some of it because my mind is all muddled up like I know I've done what you church folks say is sin. I don't know how I can get rid of it, but I hurt more than you can ever know."

Willie Washington kinda dropped the stern face he was carrying and looked like he was ready to listen to Toby.

Toby just had to say more, "Your wife said that the Lord forgives. I hope you will too. And I hope you can show me how I can get what it is that you have that makes you show mercy to even people like me."

Now I wasn't there, but I heard that Willie Washington fell down on his knees and Toby did too. They asked the Lord to come into Toby's life right then and there.

Chapter 14

The Runaway

Life at Eagle Nest Bayou Plantation without my Ethel Ann was not good. I found myself drifting over to Willie Washington's house every chance I could get. I guess it was because that was where there was more Ethel Ann than any place else because the people there were like her in every way. Her mother, Amanda Washington, had a way of talking just like Ethel Ann did. Her sister Katy Mae was very similar in appearance and had ways that reminded me of her. Even her younger sister, Missy Lou, stayed close by whenever I would go and sit on Willie Washington's front porch with him. I know that losing Ethel Ann was almost as big a blow to the Washington family as it was to me. But the thing that still bothered me most was that I was the one responsible for taking care of her, and she was carrying my baby that cause her to hemorrhage and die. Willie Washington never said so directly to me, but I think he was blaming her death on me. I would sit with him after I finished driving Ole Governor around in his polished black carriage, and we would look out over the bayou and say nothing to each other for hours on ends.

Katy Mae seemed to enjoy my visits to the Washington home. Sometimes she would sit with me like she was trying to tell me that she didn't blame me at all. I could see things in her that I liked, and she seemed to be comfortable with me too. On the other hand, I noticed that Missy Lou was still throwing admiring glances at me. But then, I could also see that she was not seeing me as a future husband but somebody more like an older brother, or even a father. That made me feel better because I had decided to ask Katy Mae to be my second wife.

Katy Mae agreed to marry me. Willie Washington seemed pleased to have her get a good husband like he knew I was. We didn't have a big wedding, but Willie made sure that a preacher married us right smart like. Kate, she didn't mind me calling her that, moved into my house and made herself at home. She was just as nice when we snuggled up in our bed for the first night.

Marrying a second wife after losing the first one was not the same as it was having the first one. But it wasn't bad either. I talked it over with Ole Governor one time when I was driving him up in his carriage to Clarksdale to look over one of those newfangled contraptions they call an automobile. Ole Governor told me that the second wife could be more loving than the first one. I wanted to differ with him, but he said that a man could look over his own past marriage and not make the same mistakes he made with his first wife. That was the one of the times Ole Governor talked seriously about his first wife. "She was a beauty and full of fun when I first married her. I met her on a trip to Baton Rouge. Her name was Vanessa, and she was one of those hot-blooded French women that looked at every thing as an opportunity for fun and adventure. She was an artist by her nature as well as her capability. She used to sit on the bank of Eagle Nest Bayou and draw scenes from the swamp and the animals and birds that were there. I still have a painting of a Blue Heron that she painted before she began to suffer from the brain problem that came on her. That's not the only picture I have of her. I got a full size one that an artist in New Orleans did. But the Blue Heron is her too,… er… I mean,… well." Ole Governor kinda stopped like he wanted to say more about the heron, but he went on. "That picture is hanging in the drawing room of Oak Hall, my present home. My wife, Melanie, doesn't seem to mind me keeping the painting, even though it represents the woman who shared my bed before her.

It seemed like Ole Governor just had to talk about his first wife. "I first noticed Vanessa's brain problem when she began to yell at her maid and the kitchen help. It just got worse over time, and I couldn't manage her tantrums. The doctors in Clarksdale and even in Memphis told me that it must have been heredity, something in her family from way back. I loved her dearly and it was tearing me up to see her that way. I would never have been able to bear seeing her locked up like they would have done if I had put her in an asylum. I did for her what I could, and when it got too bad, I… " Ole Governor couldn't go on. I knew that he was feeling a blame for something that was bothering his very soul just like he was the one that took her out in the bayou and left her there. There wasn't anything I could do or say so I just looked straight ahead and drove the carriage on to the Packard place on Isaquina Street in Clarksdale.

Ole Governor wasn't much interested in learning to drive the new Packard he was buying for himself and Ole Misses. He had the man show me how to run it. I drove it around the school yard a little after the school kids had gone home. It was the foot clutch that gave me trouble at first, but I soon got the hang of it and could get it rolling without jumping back and forth like a bucking horse that had never been broke into harness.

They had just put in the hard road from Clarksdale to Memphis, and the part of the road that run off of it to Eagle Nest Bayou Plantation was a good gravel road that the county had improved because ole Governor was the one who paid the great part of the taxes to run Coahoma County. Ole Governor made me drive slow whenever we came up on one of the houses of another plantation owner. He waved at them as they stood looking with their mouth open because they had not ever seen an automobile before. That's when I got the job for good of being Ole Governors chauffeur. Ole misses got more pleasure than Ole Governor in riding around in the new Packard and showing it off to her friends in Clarksdale. We could get to Clarksdale real quick, so Ole Misses did all her grocery shopping there.

As we were driving back through Johnstown, we noticed a man putting up posters announcing the coming to town of the Simon Diamond Tent Show. It was coming to Johnstown on Thursday of the next week. For those of you that do not know anything about Simon Diamond Shows, it is a stage show with singers and dancers the likes of many of the people in the Delta have never seen. Oh, the show boats used to pull into Friars Point for a couple of nights of showing. That's the kind of entertainment the whites of the towns around about would flock over to the river to see. Folks of my color never got to go inside the show boat so it was tent shows like Simon Diamond that we had opportunity to see. It cost a whole dollar a head to go in for a seat. Some whites in the towns would go and sit in a special section where it cost them three dollars a head to sit. That didn't matter, the Simon Diamond tent show was for people like us and we went deep into our eating money to buy the dollar ticket.

The advance man for the show came in and made arrangements with the town mayor for a place to put up the tent. Ole Doctor Stanton was the town mayor as well as the only doctor in town. He made a big show of insisting that the show could not harm the minds of the young folks in the town and the surrounding plantations. "Oh, there'll be some singing and dancing, and some of the dancers will kick up their legs where you might see some of their under pants, but the show will be all right for the family, I can assure you," the Simon Diamond advance man told Dr. Stanton. "Besides, I've reserved special seats for you and your family so you can see the show free of charge."

The main character in the show was Simon Diamond, and he was portrayed as a real sport. He had a checkered suit with a wide brim hat, and white leggings the uptown people call spats. In the show, all the girl performers played up to him, but there was a shy little one named Mary Liza that he ignored until she sang her special song. That's when he began to notice her. The show ended with Simon asking her to be his wife. There were many others who sang and danced, each one with bright colored costumes. Willie Washington's youngest daughter had listened to her mother tell about the people in Gary Indiana that went to parties and danced and had fun. Missy Lou had listened carefully. She had just turned eighteen, and she had it in her mind that it would be a good life for her. When she saw the show, on Tuesday night, she began to think that she could sing and dance just like the girls in the show, and maybe even better.

Now what I'm about to tell you is what I pieced together from the story Missy Lou told her sister Katie Mae some time later. On Wednesday morning Missy Lou slipped off from home and wandered into the tent where the owner was counting the money from the previous nights tickets sales. It wasn't unusual for girls of the town to approach the owner in hopes of getting on with the show. They say that the owner had a standard way of answering the young girls who came in to ask for a job. He simply passed them off to one of his roustabouts that put up the tent and took it down to go to the next town. "Go and talk to Jacob Martin in the cook tent," the owner told Missy Lou.

This was not an unusual thing for Jacob. It was one of the compensations he received for working with the show. He promised to help her. "Yes. I can get you on with the show," he told her, "but first let me see if you are right to be a tent show performer. Lift up your skirt and let me see your legs."

That was too much for Missy Lou. She turned and started to run away, but Jacob grabbed her and pushed her in the place where they kept the costumes. He tore at her dress, but she cried out and got away from him. It was then that Moses Walker, one of the men from Eagle Nest Bayou Plantation saw her all flushed and flustered. He knew her daddy, and he accused her of having a thing with one of the show people. Missy Lou didn't know what to do. She was so embarrassed that she didn't dare go back home to face Willie Washington and her mother.

Elizabeth Akers, one of the show girls, saw her crying and invited her into the dressing tent. "That Jacob Martin tries to do that with all the new girls who try to get a place in the show," Elizabeth told her, "You stay with me. One of our girls is going to have to leave the show to have a baby. It was that same Jacob Martin that knocked her up. There might be an opening for you to take her place. I'll do what I can to help you learn her part, if you can get Simon to take you on. In the meantime, I'll make sure that nobody will bother you while you are with me."

Missy Lou wasn't sure, but she could never go back to face her family. Elizabeth seemed to be on the up-and up so Missy Lou decided to stay with the show as long as she could.

Willie Washington and his wife assumed that Missy Lou was visiting with her sister Katy Mae at my house. Because of that, they didn't get worried about Missy Lou until all the tent show trailers had pulled out and were gone. Willie Washington walked over to my house late the next afternoon to walk his Missy Lou home in the failing twilight. When I told him that she was not with us, he got worried and asked about for her among her friends in Johnstown. The only thing he could learn was that she had left town with the tent show people. Old Doctor Stanton was unable to tell him where the Simon Diamond people had gone and what or where would be their next place for the show. I tried to console Willie Washington, but he was heartbroken. He could not understand how it was that his youngest daughter had ran away from home to take up a life with tent show people.

Chapter 15

Abduction

I can tell you, Willie Washington was doing everything he could do to find his youngest daughter. Katy Mae tried to console him by saying that Missy Lou was a grown girl who could take care of herself without a fussy daddy looking over everything she did. I could tell that my Kate was worried too, but we didn't talk about it very much since we were enjoying each other's company as newlyweds. She read scriptures to me from the Bible every night, and sometimes she would break open the book of poetry that she always seemed to enjoy. "Here's one. It might be a bit hard to understand, but it has a deep meaning. It was by a man named Longfellow that wrote something that I learned by heart."

She read it to me and I remember a certain part. It was: *Life is real, Life is earnest, And the grave is not the goal. Dust thou art to dust returnest, Was not spoken of the soul.*

I took it to mean that a man might die and be buried and his body will turn to dust, but his soul will live. That's what I could look forward to for my little Ethel Ann. And ever better, I could look forward to it for my Kate when her time should come, and my daddy and mama that I couldn't even remember what they looked like. If Missy Lou was dead or wherever she was, I could look forward to seeing her again too.

I seemed to be busy every day running Ole Misses here and there in her new Packard. Ole Governor enjoyed showing off his new automobile too, but I could tell that he was slowing down a bit. His step was not as spry, neither was he as ready to give me advice on every little thing. He just sat back most of the time and twisted the ends of his mustache like he was thinking deep. He seemed to worry about Willie Washington with his daughter Missy Lou running off to join a tent show.

"Walter Troupe," he said one day. "Do you suppose we could take some time off and find that little girl?" I allowed as we could if we did some real searching. I'd been bothered night after night worrying about Missy Lou, but there was more than that, I had been having the same nightmare almost every time I fell off sound asleep. It was not always the same dream. There were parts that were different, but it always started with me sitting up on the limb of that big cypress tree in the middle of a pool in Eagle Nest Bayou with Ole Brutus thrashing around at the bottom making leaps to try to get hold of my feet. It was the big cypress that had the eagle nest on top. Sometimes in my dream I could look up and see an empty shirt sleeve hanging down from the nest and flopping in the breeze. In other dreams, it would be a man's arm and hand that was hanging down from the side of the nest like it was motioning me to climb up. Sometimes I could see a big gold ring on the finger of the hand. I didn't want to mention the dreams to anybody. I tried to connect the dreams with the disappearance of Missy Lou, but I couldn't make any connection. They seemed to point more toward the disappearance of Ole Governor's brother, Julius Arbuckle.

Ole Governor was right. I knew I should not let my nightmares keep me from thinking about the lost Missy Lou. Maybe somebody ought to take time off and look for the tent show that kinda gobbled up that pretty girl. I would not be hard to find if a body really took the time to make a careful look.

Willie Washington was bothered something terrible. I didn't feel comfortable around him. It might have been a bit of a guilt feeling, but I was thinking that he might be blaming me for losing his oldest daughter when she miscarried carrying my baby. He might work it around in his mind that when I married Katy Mae and left only Missy Lou, his youngest, at home with him and she decided that I would never be able to marry her so she ran away to keep from being the last one at home.

Willie didn't want to talk about it. All he did was sit on his front porch in his cane-bottomed straight chair and look out over the bayou like he might see her coming walking on the water or flying down from the eagle nest that was in the big cypress.

Ole Governor took a look at Willie Washington's cotton crop and decided that something had to be done or the grass was going to take over everything. "If Willie Washington doesn't get up off his cane bottomed and get back to working his cotton, he won't have any crop at all. That means he will lose, but even worse, I'll lose because he won't be able to pay his rent. Besides that Missy Lou was a sweet kinda timid sort."

"There isn't any way of telling, but that tent show man might be holding her against her will." Ole Governor called me in and told me one Monday morning. "I'll tell you what, We'll take the Packard and drive up toward Tunica and see if we can find any of the Simon Diamond posters anywhere. If you can find out where the next show will be, I'll let you take Jody Jensen and maybe one more of the closed mouth people on the plantation and you can find where they are holding her. We'll steal her away just like that Simon Diamond man stole her away from her papa.

It didn't turn out to be that easy. First off, Simon Diamond wasn't holding her against her will. Jody Jensen found out when he nosed around the cook tent that Missy Lou was staying with the show on her own accord. He ran into the lady named Elizabeth and got the full low-down about Missy Lou. Elizabeth said, Missy Lou was a natural for the show. She said that when Simon Diamond saw those big brown eyes and that innocent round face with the bright smile, he immediately told his musicians to see if she could sing. Singing before a crowd of people was not a new thing for Missy Lou. She had sung solos in the Johnstown Church and all she had to do was learn the songs that were in the show. In no more than two days of rehearsals, Missy Lou was singing the lead part in front of everybody. Her strong voice, and her sweet smile was an instant hit with the Simon Diamond Show audiences.

"She's got a taste of what it means to be a real stage-show performer." Elizabeth Akers told Jody. "She has heard the audience applaud and stamp their feet, and yell out Missy Lou, Missy Lou. I doubt if you could ever convince her to go back to the farm and sing to cotton stalks that don't applaud or yell: Missy Lou, Missy Lou."

Ole Governor listened to Jody Jensen when he came back to us in the car and told us about his conversation with the girl, Elizabeth. He twisted his mustache ends for a minute or two and then he made up his mind. "We came up here to get Willie Washington's daughter, and, By Thunder, we will not go back to Eagle Nest Bayou Plantation without her. Here's what we will do…"

Ole Governor worked it out where we would hang around outside the main tent while the show was going on and be ready to grab Missy Lou when she had sung her part and came back to the dressing tent. "Toby Childers, you be the one to wait near the dressing tent." I forgot to tell you that as crooked as Toby Childers used to be, we agreed to let him come along with us to get Missy Lou. We figured that if he was still as sneaky and crafty as he had been in the past, he just might be the one to sneak in and get Missy Lou for us. Ole Governor had commented that it might be good to use crooks to fight crooks. Besides, Ole Toby had changed from his thieving ways; he had begun going to the Johnstown AME Church on Sundays and he was taking his whole family with him.

As I told you earlier, Toby was a little squirt that people didn't pay much notice to. He seemed to be like a mouse that would hide in a corner until a crumb of bread was dropped on the floor. Then the mouse would dash out and get the crumb and scamper back to his corner without ever being noticed all that much.

Just at the right time, Toby grabbed Missy Lou by the arm and told her that her sister Katy Mae wanted to see her. She balked a little, but he pulled her over to where the rest of us could get to her. It wasn't anytime until we had her in the back seat of the Packard and on the way home to Eagle Nest Bayou Plantation. She scratched and bit anybody she could reach while bawling and telling us that the Lord would punish us for stealing her away. When she settled down a little, she started begging us to not tell her papa and her mama what she had been doing. "My daddy would be brokenhearted if he knew one of his close kin was working in a tent show. I've heard him say a hundred times that the people who sing or dance should sing and dance for the Lord, and not for gawking senseless people to watch and think evil things about them. Please don't tell him where you found me." When she looked down at her skirt with the frills on the bottom and her blouse that opened way down from her neck, she began to cry again. "What am I going to tell my daddy about these clothes?"

It didn't matter at all. Willie Washington was so glad to see his daughter, I'm wondering if he ever noticed her clothes at all. But her mother noticed them and didn't comment. I'm guessing that Amanda Washington would not be condemning. Instead I'm guessing that she would be a little proud that her daughter was able to perform as the lead singer in a Simon Diamond Stage Show.

Chapter 16

Black Magic

It wasn't much later that year that my Kate began to show the signs of being in a family way. This pleased us all, and Willie Washington seemed to be as pleased as anyone. He was still looking for a grandson. It took him a long time to become reconciled with having a stage show performer in his family. When she first got home from singing in the Simon Diamond Tent Show Missy Lou promised to stay home and not run away again, but Willie Washington could see that she wanted something more than living on a cotton plantation all her life. He agreed for her to go back to the tent show provided she came to see him two times a year. That would work out well enough because the show moved up from New Orleans to the Delta area in the spring and again in the fall.

Ole Governor kept me on as his chauffeur and his all-round helper. I became quite good at driving him around. Driving in Memphis for the first time with him and Ole Misses was kinda scary, but that got to be old stuff after awhile. Even with the new car in the car shed, Ole Governor still enjoyed riding around the plantation in his black polished carriage. Somehow we always seemed to end up at a certain place over at the end of the bayou where we first sat down and ate the fried chicken Mandy put in the basket for his lunch. Even from that first time on, I noticed that the old man kinda reverenced that place. He would sit for several minutes without saying anything at all. At these times, he would look out over the swamp area as if he was seeing something that was not there.

"She was a beauty," he said one time when I saw a glimmer of brashness in his eyes. "She used to come to this spot and open up her painting case right here." He would point to a spot, the same spot he had so carefully walked around as if he didn't want to desecrate it by stepping on it. Sometimes he rested the palm of his hand on it like he could feel a pulse heartbeat through the dirt and the grass.

Ole Governor just had to talk. "Vanessa seemed to have a charm about her, that drew the little creatures to her," he would say, "The little birds would come down and eat crumbs at her feet when she nibbled at the lunch she brought along. There was a blue heron that always came up to the water's edge and would stand like it was posing just for her to paint him. She would talk to it in a kind of a gibberish that it seemed to understand. I watched her many times, and with each time she seemed to drift off more and more into the world of make believe. Sometimes she would not even talk to me at all. I refused to bring her to this spot, but she would beg, and sometimes she would run away from our home and sneak over here."

My old friend had more to say. "I always knew where I could find her. She would be sitting here talking to that enormous blue heron like the two of them were saying love words together. I would never get anyone to believe me, but I began to notice a change in her physique. Her legs got more spindly and she began to stretch her neck more than usual. I'm guessing she was doing it because she wanted to make the heron pose for her. But I could never be sure that wasn't some kind of metamorphous."

For me Ole Governor's one-way conversation was beginning to get a little weird I could tell that he was not enjoying the way it was coming out, but he seemed to have an inner need to say what he was saying. "I don't expect you to understand this, I'm not sure I understand it myself, but I was seeing a person I loved slowly change from a real person into something else."

Just then, we heard a faint echo-like sound that we recognized as the mating call of Ole Brutus. Ole Governor nodded his head in the direction of the sound and said, "And that's another thing too."

For me, it wasn't a comfortable situation at all. I had noticed that Ole Governor always was on the look out for a blue heron bird. Whenever we saw one flying overhead, he would make me stop the carriage so he could watch it until it went out of sight. Each time I would suggest that we had better be getting on back to the plantation main house. He was reluctant to leave like he was waiting for the heron to fly over once more and maybe swoop down and alight beside him.

On the way back to Oak Hall that day, we made a stop by Willie Washington's house. Willie was out in the field working late trying to make up for all the time he lost pining over his missing Missy Lou. He hailed us and motioned that he wanted to talk. "I've got news, and I don't know how you are going to take it," he told Ole Governor. "You know I've been saving whatever money I could get that I didn't need to feed my family. Amanda's sister up in Gary Indiana up and died and left Amanda a little more too. When it all added up it was enough for me to make an offer for the C.T. Smith place over next to Moon Lake. Old Mr. Smith has lost his wife, and his son went away to find a job up in Chicago. Mr. Smith allows that he will sell me the place outright after he picks all his cotton and gets in all his corn."

Ole Governor took the news in good order. The way of farming in the Delta had begun to change itself with the coming in of the John Deere tractors to the area. He didn't seem to mind letting Willie Washington go to his own place and start working that plot with day labor. Using day labor meant that the plantation owner paid off the workers, the tractor drivers, the cotton choppers and cotton pickers, by the day or by the week. The owners still let the people live in the plantation houses as a means of keeping a ready crew of laborers on hand. I was a kind of day-laborer myself since Ole Governor paid me a weekly wage for driving him around.

There was a nice new house that CT Smith built for his manager. There were barns and sheds also. The place was just right for Willie and Amanda since she was slowly getting over the sickness she got from nursing Toby Childers's family. Willie still had his two teams of mules and farm equipment. He would need more, but if he bought one of those John Deere tractors, he would be able to farm the whole place. If he could get his two nephews to come over and live in the two tenant houses on the back side of his place he would have enough people too. I was proud of my father-in-law and wished him well when I heard the news.

Willie was proud for another reason also. He could see Katy Mae's stomach swelling every day, and he couldn't wait to see his first grandchild. I was the one who was proudest of all because it would mean that I would have a son or a daughter to coddle that could care for me when I got too old to work.

It wasn't long after that when I began to notice that Ole Governor seemed to step around again like things were looking up for him. Even the boll weevil in the cotton didn't worry him like it had several weeks earlier. He came right out and said one morning when he got in the buggy to look over the crops at the north end of Eagle Nest Bayou Plantation, "Walter Troupe. I just learned for sure that I'm gonna be a Papa. You know a father, a daddy to a little one."

He stopped in his tracks to look at me and see if I really understood. "Did you hear, Walter Troupe? You're not the only one that's got a child on the way. Ole Misses is gonna have a son, er... maybe a daughter."

He was all jolly smiles when he told me "Melanie has been a good wife. She has wanted a child since early in our marriage. She has put up with me for the past twenty years since I married her ten years from the time I lost my first wife. We've been trying for a child from the beginning, but the Lord hasn't favored us until now."

As we rode in the carriage up to north end of the planta-tion where Tommy Nettles was having trouble keeping the grass out of his cotton rows, Ole Governor got real chummy and had a real need to talk. "Walter Troupe. The folks around here, and especially the other plantation owners, keep wondering why I don't spend more time up at Stacker's

Drug Store jawing with them about this and that. They keep wondering why I seem contented to sit and talk with my tenants and my workers like you. They call me a 'Loner,' and lots of other things too that would not be complimentary to you and the other workers on the plantation."

When Ole Governor gets in a talking mood, I have learned to be quiet and nod every now and then to show I understood. "Last night I was laying in bed all excited about what Melanie, your Ole Misses, told me about her condition. I was thinking that I'd like to tell everybody who would listen that I was gonna be a papa after all these years. I stopped to think: Now who will I tell the news to first? Then I began to realize that I didn't have anybody in Coahoma County that would show any excitement about what I would tell them. I started counting my friends on my fingers and ran out of friends before I ran out of fingers on one hand. I had a brother once, but after he got killed, er... died, er... disappeared, I didn't have anybody close that cared a whit about me, except Melanie and er... you."

It isn't good to listen or to let somebody say something that they might later wonder if it was the right thing to say so I just kept quiet. Ole Governor kept his peace for a long time while we bumped over the clods in the turn row that led to Tommy Nettle's plot. He finally blurted out: "Walter Troupe, besides my wife Melanie, I guess you are my very best friend."

I wanted to say the same thing to him, but I wanted to be careful that he wouldn't think I was being overly familiar. Lots of times, you don't have to say a word to get a feeling across to the other person. I had the thought in my head that I didn't have to say anything for him to know that I felt the same way too. It seemed to satisfy him because he didn't bring up the subject for the rest of the day.

Ole Governor invited the good Doctor McKewin to come out and hunt ducks or rabbits on his place every first Monday of the month. That was his way to get the doctor to see Ole Misses without her having to slip into his office at Clarksdale. That would keep all her friends from knowing she was in a family way until she was ready to let them know for sure. "You make sure that your Kate is here at the same time, and we will get the good doctor to check on her too," Ole Governor told me.

Katy Mae didn't feel comfortable having a white doctor look her over, but Ole Misses told her it would be alright.

Marie Leavola was the woman that served as a midwife for all the sharecropper families on all the plantations around Eagle Nest Bayou and for this end of Coahoma County. She grew up in the near part of Louisiana, and her ways were a mixture of what she had learned there from the swamp people coupled with what the people in the upper Delta area would tolerate. She always carried her little satchel of herbs and other remedies that she used whenever the patient would allow. Marie had a fierce look that scared everyone, especially the first-time mothers. When she learned that a white doctor was seeing Katy Mae, she screamed out with a screech that unnerved everybody. "It's that Walter Troupe that has his wife thinking she is an uppity woman like the whites around here. She is going to that white doctor that's gonna mess her up real bad. White doctors don't know anything about folks like us. I wouldn't be surprised if that baby don't come out with one leg missing or even something worse. Everybody knows that her sister died trying to have a baby by that worthless Walter Troupe that's been lapping up everything that white plantation owner tells him."

The word got back to my Kathy Mae and she almost fainted. Her mother was educated in a northern school and she didn't agree with the ways of the uneducated people of the Delta. Amanda Washington told my Kate that everything would be alright, but all the other women on Eagle Nest Bayou Plantation would just look and shake their heads whenever Katy Mae walked by.

"Whatever am I going to do? I can't make myself un-pregnant. I'm scared," Katie said several times. I could tell that my Kate was really scared, but I didn't know what I could do about it either. Ole Misses told Katy Mae it was nothing. "The Lord is the one who gives children, and it isn't for us to worry about what they will be."

Ole Governor was hearing all this, and he tried to comfort me so I could comfort my Kate. "You don't have to worry. Your child will be alright. I'm the one that should be worrying. You think it over, here I am coming up on my sixtieth year. I'm old when you start thinking about what it takes to make a strong child. Every once and awhile I begin to ask myself, since I'm old and getting grey-headed all over, I'm wondering if the newborn is going to come out all wrinkled with grey hair and weak eyesight." I reminded him that Abraham was over a hundred years old when he went in to Sarah who brought him Isaac.

It was just about that time when my Kate found something strange in the corner of her kitchen behind a stack of stove wood. It was a sock filled with straw that had a string tied around it to make it look like a doll. There were eyes made out of black buttons sewed on its face and a cord cinched around its waist. It had legs. But I can't really say legs because one leg was cut off much shorter than the other.

When Kate saw that there was only one leg she screamed out like she was pierced with a sharp stick. "It's a Voodoo doll!" she cried out. "Somebody is trying to put a curse on me."

I tried to console her but she wouldn't stop screaming and crying. There was no way to stop her from screaming. I ran over to her mama's house, and Amanda Washington came hobbling back with me. "It's those ignorant people who believe in that sort of stuff," she said as I helped her step up on my porch.

Kate's screaming had aroused several of the near-by neighbors. I wanted to drive them out of the house because some of them would look at the doll and nod their heads like they believed in the black-magic it represented. Amanda shushed them out and cuddled her daughter who was taller than she was in her arms and whispered kind words. This didn't seem to help, so she began to quote scripture. "The Lord quoted scripture when he was confronted with the

114

Devil on the mountain. Keep quoting scripture until the evil influence has passed."

"The Lord is my shepherd, I shall not want…" I joined in with Amanda, and soon Kate was joining in too. We went through the Twenty-third Psalms, the Lord's Prayer, and much of the Thirty Seventh Psalm that Kate always loved.

I checked over in the corner to see if I could see anything that would give me an idea of just who would have put the terrible thing there. It was then that I found another ragged doll-like object. The thing was old and dusty like it had been hidden away there for a very long time. It had a badge pinned on it like they handed out to children at Church Sunday School. It was the very same one that Ethel Ann had lost shortly after she got in a family way. This doll had a long knitting needle poked in its stomach. It took me several minutes to catch the idea what it meant.

When I realized that someone might have made the thing as a way to put a curse on my first wife, I screamed out even louder than Kate did when she first saw the doll without a leg. Amanda couldn't console me. I ran out of the house and kept running until I gave out of breath and had to slump down in the cotton field between the rows of green plants. I must have passed out because I didn't come to until later. I could hear Ole Governor talking and Ole Misses fussing over me with a wet wash cloth washing my face and wiping my forehead.

I tried to tell Ole Governor what I felt, but the words would not come out right. I wanted to tell him that I felt responsible for letting the Devil come into my house and molest my first wife, and now he was molesting my present wife.

Ole Governor was saying, and the words were confused and jumbled, but I thought I heard him say, "Devil is real. No one can deny it, but it is his agents here on earth that do his dirty work. It's people like Toby Childers…" He stopped and corrected himself, "Like Toby Childers used to be. Thank God he has embraced Jesus and has now changed his ways. It is people who do not know the Lord who do Satan's bidding."

Kate and Ole Misses were looking at Ole Governor like he might have more to say. "Walter Troupe," he continued. "Don't let yourself think for a minute that some ignorant person who had an extra pair of socks could make something like that happen. You didn't cause Ethel Ann's hemorrhage, and nothing you or anyone else can do will make the child your Kate is carrying be deformed in any way. Now you and Kate go on with your lives like this has never happened. Give me those evil fetishes and we will burn them right now."

Several of the neighboring women who came in to see what was happening backed away as if it would be bad luck to destroy the straw dolls. Ole Governor stuck them in the cookstove on the coals that were still smoldering from the breakfast cooking. They flashed up with a flame when the fire hit the straw. Several of the women said it was a purple flame that came out of the stove eye. I can't say for myself because I was holding my Kate and trying to tell her that everything would be alright.

Word got back to us the following day that Marie Leavolo fell off her porch that morning and was paralyzed from the neck down. She wasted away and died three days later. I can't say that there was any connection with that and what Ole Governor did with the dolls.

Now I didn't hear it for sure, but they say that Mandy, Ole Governor's cook, claimed that he went right back to his house and searched every corner of the kitchen that same morning.

Chapter 17

Agonizing

I don't think I ever told you, but Ole Governors house was really a mansion. It was started by his grandfather early in the days of the family as a house to live in when he was clearing the land for a cotton plantation. They say he got the land from a grant for helping General Jackson in driving out the British from New Orleans. Every year he or his son after him built up the place until it became a mansion that looked like one of those down at Natchez and Vicksburg. It had many rooms and a big ballroom that Ole Governor's daddy entertained special people that came to see him. I never got to see all the rooms, but Mandy and Essie Mae said that they had to keep them all spotless clean even though Ole Governor never had anybody come to see him.

It seemed strange that Oak Hall — that was what Ole Governor called it — never seemed to be used for anything but as a place to live in by him and his misses. Yes, Ole Misses had friends from Clarksdale that come to see her sometimes, but she never threw a party, or had a ball, or had anything that would bring a big crowd to the plantation.

I had to wonder many times why Ole Governor didn't have much truck with the people of Johnstown. He seldom talked with any of the plantation owners when he went into Stacker's Drug Store for his medicine. If there was ever any talk that concerned the farming there abouts, he would stand up and say his piece and then leave like he didn't care for small talk, or any talk at all with owners in that end of the county.

I always had to wonder about this. Maybe he was afraid someone would bring up the disappearance of his brother, and later on, his first wife too. But what grabbed my mind more than anything else was the thing about the voodoo dolls we found in my kitchen. Now I don't believe in Black Magic, and I have to say that it is from Old Nick himself. If I believed that a person could do bad things with their magic, I would have to believe in reverse miracles, or even that they had a connection with the Devil himself. Now if I believed that, I would have to think that a person could pray to the Devil and he would answer with evil the same way God would answer with good. But I didn't believe any of it.

Now I have to say that sometimes you wonder about the things that happened. Especially the thing when my Ethel Ann passed on with a miscarriage or after Marie Leavola fell off her porch about the same time of day when Ole Governor put the voodoo dolls in the fire. What worried me most was that the evil woman had put a curse on my Katy Mae. Every time I mentioned the expected baby to Kate, she would burst out crying all over again. Ole misses told her many times that she didn't have to worry. "God is the one who created the world, and God is the one who takes care of His children. And you, Kate, are surely one of His children because you have asked the Lord Jesus to come into your life long ago." She reminded my Kate of this every time she saw her.

Ole Misses and Kate seemed to have a bond between themselves. I'm thinking that it was because the two of them were carrying babies and the expected times of their births was close together. Ole Misses explained that one could not ever be sure of the day, or the week, or even the month the baby would come, but from the looks of the two of them, the birthing would be close together.

Even with all this, I was still scared. Every time I had a chance, I'd pray to God about the two expected babies. Whenever I had to wait for Ole Misses to buy her groceries at Montici's Grocery Store in Clarksdale, or when Ole Governor went into Stacker's Drug Store for his medicine, I would stand at the back of the Packard so people could not see my lips moving and pray to the Lord Almighty to drive out the evil spirit that Marie Leavolo might have put on my Kate or maybe even on Ole Misses. Sometimes I could almost see God standing at the other side of the Packard. He seemed to look worried, and I couldn't tell why. I was sure hoping that he wasn't worried over whether the Devil had more power than he had. But I was also thinking that God would never have to worry about anything since he was the master of all the universe.

My prayer was more a question than a statement. "Why would you be looking worried when you look at me, God. I'm one of your children, I don't steal, I don't hurt people, I think I'm as good as anybody else, but you still look at me with sad eyes like you see bad things in store for me." I mouthed the words to keep the people around me from calling me crazy for talking to myself. What bothered me most was that I was thinking that God was seeing bad things in store for my Kate. "God. If I've ever done anything that is worthy of punishment, put it on me and not on my Kate. And please don't punish Ole Misses along with us for my sinful acts, whatever they are."

Now I can't say that God was there in front of me in the flesh, but it sure seemed that He was there still looking sad like He would like for me to make amends for something I had done. He looked like He wanted to remind me of that day I ran out into Eagle Nest Bayou and was so mad with him for letting Ethel Ann die that I told Him I didn't believe in Him any more. I told Him that if that was what He did to people, I didn't need Him anymore.

I'll tell you all, when you really meet with God, you had better be ready to get yourself all cleaned up because He can look at you and see any of the ugly spots on your soul of the hate you might have in your heart for Him, or for anyone else for that matter.

"God. If I cursed you, I didn't really mean it. I was just heartbroken for losing my Ethel Ann." No matter what I said, in my mind, He was still looking at me kinda sad like. I began to see, or I think that I was seeing, that He wasn't mad at me, He was sad to see a body who was hurting like I was. "God I…" It was then that I was reminded of King David and how he prayed after he had sinned with that woman Bathsheba. I always felt sorry for King David because he knew he had sinned. I guess I will always remember what he prayed. "Have mercy on me O God according to Thy tender mercies. Purge me with hyssop and I shall be clean." Now I didn't know where there might be any hyssop, I don't know what it really is, but the Lord can pull hyssop out of the air if that is what He wants to do like He made water come out of the rock when the Children of Israel had parched throats and were dying of thirst in the wilderness. I was hoping that he would pour it all over me to clean me "White as snow" like King David said.

I know the people passing by who happened to see me must have thought I was crazy. In my mind I could see that the Lord had changed from looking sad, and He kinda grinned at me like He knew I was asking for His forgiveness. When I saw that He was smiling, I fell to my knees and thanked Him. That was when I heard a nasty comment from someone on the street, "That's the Arbuckle chauffeur from Eagle Nest. There must be something in the water down there that makes them all act crazy. First it was the crazy brother that disappeared, then it was that Arbuckle wife that went mad. Now one of the hired help is kneeling down in the dust like he has lost his mind."

I really didn't care because it looked like the Lord was grinning at me and was going to make everything right.

Chapter 18

Drought

Some people don't know how good it feels when you have cleansed yourself of all the bad things you might have done. It feels like you have just come out of a pool of clear water after you have lathered up with sweet smelling soap. Even the lye soap the women make with leftover grease and potash is good, but when you get to use the white store-bought soap, or better still the soap that comes out of the orange wrapper that has a gentlemanly smell about it, you feel real clean. That's the way I felt when I raised up from kneeling down behind the Packard at Stacker's Drug Store.

Ole Governor seemed to notice the difference in my feeling as soon as I opened the door for him to get into the car. "You look like you got a weight of worry off your mind," he told me as we headed back toward Eagle Nest Bayou Plantation. It was a beautiful day with a clear blue sky up above us. I told Ole Governor that with the fair sky and the sun shining down making all the grass green and lush, it should be a good growing season. More than that, I told him that I wasn't worried anymore about Kate and the baby that was due about any time now, and that I knew it would be whole and healthy.

There was a warm breeze up from the south, and it warmed my skin and my feelings as well. I was thinking that it would be good if the weather stayed that way for the next forty days. It would be a good beginning in life for our baby that was soon to come. I don't know why forty days came to my mind because I realize now that you need a little rain every now and then to make you appreciate the warm easy days. I'm guessing that I remembered Miss Molly reading about Noah in the Ark when it rained forty days and forty nights without stopping. It hit me kinda funny like, and I couldn't help asking Ole Governor why did he think the Lord brought a flood on the people back then.

"They were evil. The lord regretted the way His creation were acting," Ole Governor pointed out, "and He decided to destroy them all. The scriptures say that it grieved the Lord to see what He was seeing." I could readily understand that because I was thinking that it grieved Him when he saw the way I had acted.

I began to think what it would be like if it rained forty days and forty nights here in the Delta. It is flat here just like the top of the pool table up in Haggard's store where the men hang out on Saturday night. I looked out over the flat cotton fields and reasoned it out that if it rained that much here, all the cotton land would be covered and the bayous would overflow and let those big alligators out to chase the people who were trying to get away from the flood. Then I began to think what it would be like if it didn't rain. If the clear blue sky was there all the time for forty days and forty nights or even longer, if it didn't rain it might be just as bad as a flood.

Well that's just what happened. It didn't rain.

But things were still looking up. My Kate gave birth to a little girl. We named her Caroline Amanda. She was whole and beautiful. I can't tell you how good it was to hear her crying for the first time. Babies can't talk when they are first born. All they can do is bawl to let you know that they are alive, and that they think they are really somebody that needs attention. But the sky stayed blue, and the warm breeze blew in from the south that made everybody talk about what a nice spring it would be.

Spring came and went, and the sky still stayed clear. Ole Governor had his field hands wait a little bit before he would let them put in the seed, hoping there would be some rain to moisten the soil. Now if you plowed real deep, you could get down to where there was dirt that didn't turn to dust the moment the plow turned it over. He finally had his people plant, but all the other plantation owners had planted in the dry dirt or were doing like him and waiting.

I have to tell you that when the little cotton shoots finally came up they were scraggly with long gaps in the rows. There wasn't much use to worry about grass growing in amongst the plants because the grass was having just as hard a time growing as the cotton plants.

There was a light rain that came in late afternoon one day. It wasn't much more than enough to settle the dust and it dried up almost as fast as it fell. Ole Governor wasn't the only one that was hurting.

Now everybody didn't take a daily paper, but Ole Governor would have me drive the Packard into Clarksdale and get a copy of the Memphis Commercial Appeal every Thursday. I could read enough to see that everybody in the Delta all the way down past Vicksburg were having the same weather, or lack of rain like we were having.

Ole Governor's baby came not much later than our Caroline Amanda. It was a girl too, and I have to say she was beautiful with blue eyes and little dimples. Ole Misses named her Frances Annabelle after her grandmother. I wouldn't want to say it in front of Ole Governor, but Frances Annabelle Arbuckle didn't even come close to looking as good as our Caroline Amanda.

Even with a new baby in the house, Ole Governor seemed to be distressed every time I picked him up in the black polished carriage to look at his crops, or when he wanted me to drive him to Clarksdale in the Packard to talk to his banker.

Now here's something I never realized. Even though he owned a big plantation and lived in a big house and bought a new car every year, Ole Governor still had money problems. He explained to me one day as I was driving him to Clarksdale to see his banker. "You may not know it, but just about every planter in the Delta operates on borrowed money. They borrow the money to buy the seed and fertilizer. Paying the help is the biggest expense. Whenever I hand out furnish money to the sharecroppers, it's money I borrowed from the Citizens Bank or Production Credit to make the crop."

It took a lot of guts for Ole Governor to tell me that if he had a crop failure, he would have no way to pay back the loan for making the crop. "It doesn't help to be a shareholder, or part-owner in a bank, because the bank is lending borrowed money too. They get it from their depositors, or sometimes they get loans from other big banks in Memphis or St Louis. Your banker may be your best friend, but if he is in hock to other banks, he is not going to be able to carry you along a year or two until you can come up with the money you owe." Ole Governor looked like he was worried sick over the prospects of having the bank take over his plantation.

It worried me too, because if Ole Governor had money problems, it would mean that all his tenants would have problems too.

Over the period of the next six months to a year, Ole Governor had to sell off parts of his plantation to keep the banks from taking all of it. I was glad that he was able to keep the part that had Oak Hall and the house he had built for me and Eth, that now Kate and me and Caroline stayed in. He had to give up living in Oak Hall because of the extra expense for the kitchen help and the money it took to keep it painted and in good repair. He left it the way it was except he boarded up the windows and doors on the bottom story. All this, but he was able to build himself a nice house for himself and Ole Misses, and Frances Annabelle. Too, he was able to keep the part of his plantation at the south end with the cemetery and where he always went to eat his fried chicken lunch.

It really hurt me to see Ole Misses have to move to a smaller home, but she didn't seem to mind it at all. She had her Frances Annabelle to coddle and love. You would think that Ole Governor was in heaven having his wife and little girl without having to worry about a big house, the crops, and the grass in the cotton. He didn't have Mandy to make him a basket of fried chicken, but Ole Misses did things even better. She would make egg salad along with fried bologna sandwiches.

I got me a job at the cotton seed oil mill in Johnstown that paid enough for me and my Kate and my Caroline to live on. Sometimes I would buy beef steak from Jimmy Lee's Market and take it over for Ole Misses to cook for the man who had been so good to me. My Kate would go with me, and she would sit with Ole Misses and talk like they were sisters while Caroline and Frances played on the floor together.

I found it hard to call Ole Misses anything but Ole Misses, but she insisted that I call her Melanie just like Kate was doing. It was hard at first, but it came easy after a while. Even with that, I couldn't make myself call Ole Governor anything but Ole Governor.

The old man still liked to go out to that special spot on the bank of the bayou near the willow tree. I kinda felt that it was the place where the remains of his first wife was buried, but I was wrong. One day when the wind was blowing a warm soft south breeze, he kinda opened up like he had never done before. "Walter Troupe. I know you have wondered many times why I always liked to come to this place to sit and just meditate."

I had to nod, because it has been on my mind ever since we first went to the place. It was the way he always stopped and got quiet for a little while before he would open up the basket of fried chicken Mandy always fixed for him.

"You probably think that this is the place where I buried my first wife Vanessa. She is not here. I have to say I don't know where she is." Ole Governor waited for that to sink in. "I told you that she was deranged. She was losing her mind and I could see what it would be like in the next month and the next year. I felt sorry for her, but there was noting I could do. I certainly couldn't see her taken to an asylum where they would have locked her in a room with padding to keep others from hearing her scream."

On previous times, Ole Governor seemed to not want to give any details because I'm thinking it was an embarrassment for him. This time he talked freely like he was talking to a dear friend, and I knew he felt like I was a dear friend.

"It was half past four o'clock in the afternoon when I missed her. I knew how she liked to go out to that special place and talk to the animals. There was an enormous blue heron. It was as tall as she was. It would pose for her to draw or to paint as if it knew exactly what she wanted."

Ole Governor didn't rush himself because I could tell that he had a long story to tell. His manner was such that I could tell it was good for him to get it out of his bones.

"That heron would chatter and she would chatter back in a language that was much the same. When I saw the two of them talking like they were saying love words to each other, I stepped back behind this tree and watched." Ole Governor pointed to the big willow on the bank of the bayou.

In my mind I could see an old man with a white mustache peeking from behind the tree, but I could also imagine his distress seeing the love of his life chattering like a wild bird. He is my friend, and I hurt for him like it was me instead of him that was losing a love.

"Walter, I watched for a long time, then I saw that great blue heron wade back into the bayou. I swear it looked like he motioned for her to follow." Ole Governor faltered here like he didn't want to go on. He swallowed once or twice and then said. "Right there before my eyes, my Vanessa followed right behind that blue heron into the swamp. I could see him looking back at her like he was expecting her to step right where he stepped. "

I waited for Ole Governor to go on, but he had stopped like that was the end of the story. He folded up the little table cloth we always spread on the grass when we ate the fried chicken, or later on, the bologna sandwiches. I couldn't help wanting to know more. Did she come back? Did she drown? Did a cotton mouth, or maybe Ole Brutus get her?

Ole Governor read my mind. He kept talking, "I would like to tell you that I ran and got her and took her back home. I did not. I know you are wondering if her body floated up and I buried her right here on this spot. No. I didn't. I will tell you that before I left the spot, I saw two blue herons flying up out of the bayou way over at the end. They flew together wing to wing like two lovers."

My first thought when I heard it was that Ole governor had gone mad like he said Vanessa had done. Again he read my mind. "Walter. I haven't gone mad. I know that Vanessa must have stepped into a sink hole or in quick sand, and got sucked out of sight. But at the time, I couldn't bring myself to have somebody drag every deep hole in the bayou. It was much easier to tell everyone that she just disappeared, which in fact, was the case. The Sheriff came out and poked around a little, but he wasn't too interested in finding a woman that everybody said had gone mad."

Ole Governor tried to show that he was satisfied with his explanation, but he wasn't doing a good job of it. I couldn't be sure he was telling me the whole story. It looked like he was wanting to say more. If that were to be true, I decided that in time, a day would come when he would tell me more. He did say he had buried Vanessa's painting case on the spot as a memorial to her.

Chapter 19

Eagle Nest Refuge.

Work in the cotton-seed-oil mill wasn't too bad. It kept me and my family going. But I have to say that my father-in-law Willie Washington turned out to be a good businessman farmer. When everybody else was borrowing money from the bank to make a crop, Willie Washington cut back on his planting and weathered the storm, except it was not a storm, but a drought. He didn't have big fertilizer bills, and he had saved the seed from the previous year. He didn't have big day-labor costs because his two nephews worked their own sharecrop and helped him out too so he made out alright.

The following year had a good growing season. He bought a tractor, and I taught his nephews how to drive it. You might say that Willie Washington became a gentleman farmer well respected in the farming community around Johnstown. And too, his Missy Lou had become a big star in New Orleans. Not only did she have a pretty smile and a pleasing voice, she had a business head on her shoulders. She saved her money and bought into one of the restaurant night-clubs there. With the profits, she was able to send money back to Willie Washington to invest in cotton land in Coahoma County that he now manages for her. Her chauffeur drives her up from New Orleans to see her family from time to time. I don't think she will ever take a husband. I hope it's not because of missing out on me as her first love.

You might think that an oil mill worker would not be able to be a friend with anybody but the working class of people, but it was not true. I had Ole Governor as a friend, and I was a special part of the Willie Washington family since I brought my father-in-law a grand baby. I was very contented, except for one thing. I still had those nightmares about the eagle nest in the big cypress tree. I could still see that arm hanging out like a man had climbed up into it to get away from Ole Brutus. Sometimes the arm would hang like the owner of it was dead or lifeless.

There were other times when the arm would motion to me like it wanted to lure me up into the nest. I never told Ole Governor about my dreams because I didn't want to grieve him by letting him think I was seeing his brother's arm waving down at me from up there in the tree. But that was what I was thinking.

There would be times I would work hard and sweat there in the oil mill climbing ladders to check on pipes, or pulling ropes to haul up barrels. The climbing and pulling caused me to think that one day I would climb up that big cypress and look to see if there were any rags or maybe bones that would prove Ole Governor's brother climbed up there and died.

Finally, I made up my mind to climb that big cypress and see what was might be in the nest. I got me a set of spikes and ropes to see if I could make the climb. Now just like Ole Governor didn't want to tell about his Vanessa, I didn't want to tell about my dream for fear people would think I was crazy. Getting the row boat back through the brush and swamp bushes was the hardest part.

With a hand full of long spikes and a hammer hanging down from my belt, I made the first limb. Ole Brutus sensed everything that went on in the thickest part of the bayou, and you can bet he was there on the knoll at the bottom of the cypress snarling at me for invading his territory. I don't know if he was remembering that I was one that baited the hook to catch him that day. Even though I might be able to climb up to the nest, I knew that I wouldn't be able to get back in the boat as long as that monster was down there waiting for me.

It wasn't easy hanging on to one spike and trying to drive in another one higher up too. When I got up right beneath the nest, it was a big job to break away the sticks and firewood-like rods and reeds that the eagles took up there for years and years of raising young. I had to push my way through a narrow hole that seemed to close up behind me. All that was bad enough but fighting off those big birds that attacked me for ruining their home, was something too. They would fly up a hundred feet or so and then dive down on me like I was wild game that they wanted to catch and take home to their young, except I was already right there with the young birds that were all naked without feathers. They didn't look like they would ever stop diving down with those big claws that scratched my face and my arms and legs. I found part of an old shirt the eagles had used to make their nest and wrapped on my head to try to shield myself from the terrible claws. Even the young birds had claws that dug into my legs when they climbed up on me.

I'm guessing that the parent birds seeing their young clinging to me made them think that I wasn't going to molest them. They quit diving at me but they set up a circle around the tree, sometimes alighting on the edge of the nest, and sometimes going to another tall cypress that was on the far edge of the pool.

I was trapped with that big gator down below and the two big eagles soaring above to decide whether they would attack me again. All this commotion almost caused me to forget my reason for climbing the Eagle Nest cypress in the first place. I noticed that there were small bones everywhere in the nest. They were mostly bleached dry, but I could tell that some of them were from small game the eagles brought up to feed their young. Almost every bone looked like it could be a finger bone or maybe an arm bone of a human. I began to look and see if any of them might still have that big gold ring that Jody Jensen was always talking about. While I was up there wondering what I was going to do, I happened to look down to the water below. If I squinted my eyes and waited till a cloud shaded the sun, I could see the outline of a plowshare right there at the bottom of the pool. I couldn't be for sure, but it looked like I was seeing a second plowshare down there too. I decided that it was the sun that was making my eyes play tricks on me. The plowshare was all rusted, but if you had any imagination you could see the part where the handles would be attached if they hadn't been rotted away.

I have to tell you I was up in that nest for a long time. I knew that my Kate was worried to death because I told her I wouldn't be gone very long. There were two sunrises before I was missed from my job, but Kate had already gotten people out looking for me. Jody Jensen remembered that I had mentioned the nest in the big cypress, and he got a boat and pushed through the brush until he saw Willie Washington's boat at the foot of the tree. He had brought his shotgun with him and after peppering Ole Brutus with bird shot from both barrels, the big gator paddled off to the far side of the pool. It seemed to know that Jody had more shells for his gun, so he didn't come very close until Jody could help me get down and in my own boat.

Jody was full of questions, but when I told him that there was nothing but varmint bones in the nest he seemed satisfied. I didn't tell him about seeing the plow share or the scrap of blue shirt.

It took several days for the claw scratches on my face to heal. My Kate made me go to see Dr. Stanton to get a tetanus shot. I'm not sure she will ever forgive me for trying such a foolhardy stunt as climbing up the tree. I could never tell her exactly why I did it. She loves me, and it was not hard for her to forget.

But Ole Governor didn't forget. He hobbled all the way over to my house to ask about it. He sat down in the cane bottom chair that Willie Washington gave me and Kate after we got married. There was no getting around it, he wanted to talk about the big cypress.

"You just had to find out for yourself didn't you," he started out looking at me with his head coked to the side like he did the time I came back all wet from my forced swim in the Mississippi. "You wouldn't believe natural reasoning, and you needed proof."

I wasn't sure if he was jesting, or that he was as riled up. "You believed that your old friend, the one you call Ole Governor, killed his brother Julius and dumped his body in the big pool at the foot of the big cypress in Eagle Nest Bayou?" He said it like it was a question more than a statement. "The water is clear this time of year and I guess you saw that plow share in the bottom of the pool."

Now I am an honest man, and there isn't any way that I can lie without it showing in my eyes. Ole Governor knew that, and he kept looking at me down the side of his nose to show me he wouldn't tolerate any quibbling.

"I see you've got that scrap of blue shirt that you had tied around your head to keep off the eagles. I know it must have come from the eagle nest up in the cypress." I had to nod because there wasn't any use to try to evade the truth. I was hoping that Ole Governor wouldn't evade the truth either. It wasn't that I wanted to prove that he was the one who did away with his brother, I was really trying to prove that it wasn't him that did that bad thing. There wasn't any way I could get it across to him as long as he was suspecting the other thing.

"You and I have been friends for a long time." When I heard that, I got ready for him to tell me that we were no longer friends. I thought I knew him well enough to know that he wouldn't harm me even if I should find out that he killed his brother, but I wasn't too sure. After he told me about seeing his Vanessa walk out into the swamp, I began to wonder if he had finally gone mad himself.

"You are still my friend, my very best friend," he said, "And I think it is time I tell you the full story about my brother's disappearance."

Ole Governor told me how he came back to Eagle Nest Bayou Plantation after serving as an aide to Old Governor Alcorn in the state capital of Jackson. "I never was a governor. I worked there after I got out of the University Law School. My friends there called me Governor as a joke, and I guess I liked the nickname. It seemed to stick after I got back to Eagle Nest Bayou Plantation. I never corrected anyone who might have thought I had been the state's chief executive."

I could tell the old man was getting relief by admitting the truth. He seemed more relaxed, and he pulled his chair over closer so he could clap his hand on my knee from time to time when he thought he had made a point. "It was a cold day in November when I got home from my stint in the capitol and I found the plantation in a mess. Brother Julius had wasted away all the assets. After his Creole woman left him, he spent more time with a bottle in his hand lying back in the recliner before the fireplace reading books about life on the sea than he did overseeing the crops. I went over the account books with him, and he couldn't explain where all our money went."

It looked like Ole Governor was telling the truth because he seemed to be hurting with every word that came out of his mouth. "Our father left everything to Julius even though he was the youngest. There was no official will. They didn't probate estates back in those days, but my father gave Julius the big golden ring to show that he was bequeathing the estate to him."

"I loved my brother," Ole Governor went on, "and I was disheartened to see what a mess he made of things. I railed at him. He bristled up and railed back at me. He acted like he would hit me with his whisky bottle. That's when I yelled out and told him if he did, I'd take it away from him and beat his brains out." The old man was talking fast as if he wanted to get it all out before he got tired and had to quit. "Julius put the bottle down and began to sob saying that he was never cut out to be a farmer. He wanted a life on the sea. From his childhood onward he had read all the books about Pirates, and Privateers, and the naval officers who chased them. When I was twelve, and he was ten, he made me promise that if he died first, I would see that he had a burial at sea. "If you can't get me to the ocean, then sink me down in the deepest hole in Eagle Nest Bayou" was what Julius told his brother Ole Governor kept on talking, "I loved my brother, and it hurt me to see him suffering with his need for the bottle. I would have done anything to help him. In his drunken state, he told me that he was going down to New Orleans and catch the first ship that would take him on as a deck hand. I knew he didn't mean it. I had heard that threat from him many times when he got old enough to buck our father. But this time he seemed more resolute than ever before. He took off the big gold signet ring and put it on the ring finger of my left hand. 'Eagle Nest Bayou Plantation is yours. I don't want any part of it.' Those were his last words to anyone in this world. He simply went outside got on his horse and rode away."

Ole Governor stopped his story long enough to say that his threat to Julius when his brother brandished the bottle was the biggest mistake he has ever made. "It didn't mean anything to him, but it would plague me the rest of my life. I wish I could have retracted it because some of the servants overheard the part about *Beat your brains out*."

Ole Governor told how he heard a horse whinny almost immediately after Julius rode away. "When I heard his horse whinny, I knew something had gone wrong. Julius had a habit of jumping the gate rather than stopping to open it. It was easy to see that horse was unable to make the jump and Julius was thrown against the fence post."

I could see that Ole Governor was getting tired, but he kept on saying "Maybe it was because Julius was staggering drunk and didn't handle the horse right, but he ended up with a big gash in his scalp with part of his brains showing through the fractured skull. There was blood all over his upper body, and he wasn't breathing when I finally got to him. I brought him inside, but when I put my ear to his chest, I couldn't hear a heartbeat. That's when I got blood all over my hands and clothes that the servants later saw. Old Abraham, my father's personal valet, told all the household help that they should never mention what they heard or what they saw that terrible evening when all this happened. I think they were more loyal to Abraham than they would have been to me. Even so, none of them ever breathed a word to anyone who would have called in the authorities. Old Abraham went to his grave with what he thought was a secret that would convict me if the matter ever came to trial," Ole Governor said. His words showed that he was sorry that he had not returned from the university earlier and taken over the plantation sooner. "The ring should have been mine in the first place because I was the first born. My aged daddy got angry and put it on Julius's hand because I stayed in the state capitol rather than come back to be a farmer. I guess I spent more time running down to see Vanessa at New Orleans than I did coming back to the Delta to see him. The old man claimed I thought more of a French woman than I did my own daddy."

The one I now call my friend had more to say, "My father told me several times that I should come home and marry one of the society girls he could get for me out of Clarksdale or Natchez. 'You could set yourself and her up in this big house and be a real Mississippi Planter,' my daddy told me. I told Dad that the life he described was not the kind of life I wanted. He got angry, and we had a row. That's when he called in Julius and gave him the signet ring. He knew that Julius was worthless, but he chose him out of spite."

Ole Governor kept on talking, "I had all sorts of thoughts. I was sad to see it end that way, but I knew that if anyone saw Julius's head wound, they would have surely attributed his death to my vengeance and my desire to remove all doubt as to who owned the plantation."

Ole Governor seemed relieved that I wasn't doubting his word at all. They way he described it, I could get a hint of the feeling he might have had back on that night many years ago. He told me he panicked. He said he knew that some of the kitchen help heard him vow to kill his brother. *Beat his brains out* was the words he had used. Thinking that everyone would be convinced he had killed his brother, he knew he had to conceal the death.

"But there was more to it than that," Ole Governor told me. "I had promised Julius that I would bury him at sea, or at least in the deepest hole of Eagle Nest Bayou. I needed a weight to sink the body. The plowshare and the chain were in the boat. I guess Julius was going take them to the farmer on the other side of the bayou to swap for another bottle. I knew I would have a hard time making people believe that Julius was killed when his horse failed to make the jump.

Anyone who saw the nature of the wound on his head would have remembered my threat and be convinced that I had indeed *Beat his brains out.* that night."

Ole Governor seemed to get tired from too much talking, but he labored on. "Convincing everyone that I didn't kill my brother would have been impossible. I worked up in my mind that a disappearance would be the best story. I fabricated the tale about Julius's leaving in the boat to sell the farm equipment. Getting the boat with the plowshare through the swamp bushes was the most difficult part for me, even more difficult than getting the body over the side of the boat to sink in the deep pool beside the eagle-nest cypress. I said a short eulogy and pushed the body over the side. Ole Brutus attacked me while I was dumping Julius in the deep pool. I got away from him, but he snapped at my hand when I was putting the scrap from Julius's shirt on a bush to make it look like he was devoured by the alligators. Brutus almost pulled me out of the boat, but I finally got away. That's when I lost this finger that had the ring Julius gave me before he rode away. I guess the ring is still in that alligator's belly to this day. Even with the loss of a finger, I felt secure with what I had done. If people should have ever questioned the matter, they would have found the plowshare in the pool and the ring in that alligator's belly and would have attributed the disappearance to Old Brutus."

Now I have to tell you that what Ole Governor told me about the disappearance of his first wife, and his brother was hard to believe. If you had been there and had seen the pain in he was having to admit to a lie about his stint as Governor, and the loss of his first wife and his brother, I'm sure you would have believed him like I did. I'm glad now that I didn't let Jody Jensen split open Brutus and get the ring that day we caught him with that big fish hook. Ole Governor told me that he would rather have the mystery of disappearance survive than to have to recount again the facts of the night of his death.

Chapter 20

Ole Governor's Last Days

Ole Governor lived on for three more years after that. I visited him often. There wasn't much I could do for him and his family that he wasn't able to do for himself. Even so, I took him beefsteak for Melanie to cook for him every single Saturday that came.

He passed on in his sleep after a peaceful day watching his Frances play hopscotch with my Caroline. I'm pleased to say he didn't have a stroke. He had been going to Stacker's Drug Store for his high blood pressure medicine for as long as I can remember, and being paralyzed was something he had always dreaded. I will always be indebted to him for showing me how to live.

Just before he died, he called me in to his bedside. In almost inaudible words he spoke as if it was something he had to say. "My friend, I can't go to meet my maker without telling you the whole story about my first wife. Remember, I told you she wandered off into the bayou and disappeared. That was true, but she always returned dripping wet with no effort to explain. I'm guessing she wanted to drown herself, but she just couldn't go through with it."

The old man seemed to be pleased that I was sharing his feelings. "I loved my Vanessa dearly, almost as much as I loved the one you call Ole Misses," he continued. "It tore my heart to see her in that mental state. Like a wild animal, she was. So many times, she asked me to take her life. When I refused, she vowed to do it herself."

Ole Governor seemed to revive a bit as he found that he could tell the truth about Vanessa's disappearance. He raised up from his pillow and blurted out the rest. "As much as I wanted to please her, I just couldn't find ways to do it. I even hid all the things that she would have used, my pistol, the rat poison, and the kitchen knives. I came in from inspecting the crops one day and found my bureau drawer open and my Heinkel razor missing. She was gone, but I knew where she would be. When I reached that special place on the edge of the bayou, the buzzards were already circling."

I've never seen Ole Governor cry, but his eyes were wet with tears. I wiped them away with my old red handkerchief, and he seemed to appreciate it. He eased back on his pillow and managed to get out the rest of the story. "Walter, you said you saw a plow share in the water of the clear pool in the bayou. If you had looked real closely, you would have seen two plow shares. I buried my Vanessa in the bayou just like I had buried Julius some time previously. If you should remember how strange I may have acted when we sat at the water's edge and ate Mandy's chicken, it was that same place where I had found Vanessa's body with my razor still in her hand. She had slashed her wrists and bled to death. I hear tell that although it is painful, it is an easy way to go."

Ole Governor managed to get out a few more words before the end came. "I loved that woman. She was like a little child. And the way she talked to that blue heron, made me think she was more animal than she was human. When I saw the two herons flying together, I...." He never finished the sentence.

They let me speak at his funeral services. I said many flowery things, but I know that he would have appreciated the way I closed my speech. It was:

The man I have always known as Ole Governor is resting up in Heaven right now. He would like for all who knew him to be there with him some day. And you can. You can go there and be with him if you will accept the salvation God has provided for you. The scriptures say: 'For God so loved the world that He gave His only begotten Son, that whosoever believeth on Him will not perish but have everlasting life.'".

138

Melanie Arbuckle the one I always called Ole Misses, died of influenza about a year after Ole governor passed on and left her little girl an orphan. It had been a hard winter. They said that the flu epidemic spread all over the country killing a quarter of the population in some towns. My Kate tended Melanie as best she could while keeping Frances Annabelle and my Caroline. The terrible disease got Kate too. It was hard to see my Kate pass away, but she left me a little girl that is much like her in every way. In fact, she left me with two little girls to take care of.

Melanie Arbuckle passed away before my Kate. The two of us took in Frances Annabella like she was our own. Some of the whites in Johnstown objected, but Melanie left a letter saying that if she should die she wanted me and Kate to adopt Frances so her little girl could be reared with her little friend, Caroline. It's in the court right now, but our lawyer thinks he can make it work out where the judge will grant Melenie's wishes.

It took them about six months to getting around to the official reading of Ole Governor's will. The provisions of it surprised almost everybody, and me most of all. Ole Governor had investments that were untouchable until his death. He was able to save his old home, Oak Hall. He left it and a sizable amount to me and Katy Mae provided we adopt his Frances Annabelle. Kate and I went through the adoption process about a month after Ole Misses passed away. Of course, now with Kate gone, it all fell upon me to take care of my own Caroline and now my Frances Annabelle. Since we had also gotten the home he built for himself and his wife, Ole Misses, we chose to stay in the smaller home since it suited our needs. We locked up Oak Hall while we were waiting to decide what we would do with it.

Missy Lou came up from New Orleans to attend Kate's funeral. She never went back. She was still the big eyed, round face smiling little girl I remembered when she shot glances my way at Johnstown Church. I suppose she never got over losing her first love to her sisters. She said she loved me then, and it was easy for her to love me again. We were married after a reasonable time following Kate's death. We now live in a nice home at the end of Eagle Nest Bayou. Our two little girls, Caroline Amanda and Frances Annabelle love each other like sisters. One is fair and the other is dark, but they are ours to love and cherish. Missy Lou is showing signs of being in a family way. Her daddy, Willie Washington, is happy as a squirrel with a corn crib of its own with the thought that Missy Lou's expected baby would be the grandson he always wanted.

End